A Matter of Taste

A Crown & Heart Novella

Book 1.5

By

Nikki Davenport

Library of Congress Control Number: 2024901416

ISBNs

Ebook: 979-8-9890545-6-5

Print: 979-8-9890545-9-6

Cover design by GetCovers.

Published by Granite Clover Publishing, LLC

www.nikkidavenport.com

First Edition: November 2023

Chapter One

Maxine

S O, SHE WAS REALLY doing this.

Maxine Abernathy tightened her grip on the wheeled garment rack and hoped like hell no one else in the elevator could hear her pounding heart. Her head was also pounding—the damn pain relief tablets she'd swallowed had yet to take effect.

Anytime now would be great.

Doing her best to inhale in a deep, controlled manner to center herself, Maxine let her eyelids flutter closed for a moment. Sleep had been impossible. Her stomach had been in a tense knot for days, and she was on edge. It almost drove her back to coffee, despite being caffeine-free for years.

She only had one shot at this, and everything was riding on it. Although she'd designed a fabulous ensemble for the new Queen's big day, Maxine's stomach did a slow, nauseating roll.

Being on retainer as the Queen's personal stylist was a dream come true, and here it was, within her grasp. She'd done the work, paid her dues, and crafted a modern, kick-ass look for the young woman who would take the Kingdom of Lytua's crown today.

All eyes of the small island nation would be glued to the media as Khara Therin took her oath. Armchair fashionistas would pick apart every detail of her attire.

Pleasing everyone with this task was hopeless, but if the Queen liked it.... Maxine just wanted to strike the proper tone.

A glance at the display panel showed there were four floors to go. Maxine lifted her chin and squared her shoulders, determined to project cool competence, as if she did this sort of thing every day. Dressing the monarch? *Pfft, no big deal.*

At her side, her assistant Dennis cleared his throat for the umpteenth time and tugged at his collar. The young man was barely holding it together; he had that wild-eyed look of someone running on too much caffeine and not enough sleep.

"Steady," Maxine whispered—as much to herself as to Dennis. "The hard work is done. We got this." His head bobbed in agreement.

Once she got through this part, she'd take something stronger for her headache, go to bed, and wait for the reviews to come in.

A cheery tone sounded overhead, and a smooth voice announced their arrival on the eleventh floor. The elevator doors slid open with a swish, and Maxine gathered herself.

Time to do this.

A harried-looking aide was waiting to greet them with a bright smile. "Ms. Abernathy, Mr. Sweeting—this way, please."

Dennis had offered to steer the rack, but Maxine had put him in charge of the accessories instead. They followed the aide as she ushered them to a waiting area outside the Queen's office. They unpacked their tools and supplies onto the table that had been set up for them. Maxine reminded Dennis—and herself—to breathe.

Her training took over, edging out the nerves. Dennis had been her apprentice for close to two years now. They worked well together and had performed this dance many times. However, they had never done it with such a VIP before. The air was electric with excitement as Guards and other staff members hurried by.

Maxine unzipped the garment bag and removed the dress with great care. She held it aloft to admire it. A dazzling number in citrine with seed pearls at the peplum hem and flounced sheer sleeves. The fitted skirt flared out into a mermaid silhouette; Maxine knew it was going to look positively stunning.

"It's perfect," Dennis sighed. Maxine's heart swelled. They grinned at one another.

She'd poured her entire soul into this project and felt thrilled with how her vision had come to life. With an irrepressible smile, Maxine spun around and let out an *oof* when she collided with a hard body and lost her balance. Her feet tangled with the other person's. With a cry, Maxine flung out her hand to grab whatever she could to halt her fall, even as she went ass-over-teakettle. Her fingers closed on the table skirt. She went down hard, with the upended garment rack falling on top of her and whomever she'd crashed into. The sound of breaking dishes echoed in the hallway.

Voices swirled around her, asking if she was alright as hands pulled the rack off her and upright.

Maxine attempted to push herself up to her knees from where she'd gone sprawling, but she slipped and ended up face down in fabric. Strong arms closed around her waist and assisted when she tried again. She'd landed on top of a solid man who was frowning at her. Where had he come from?

He had the most beautiful eyes—an unusual brown with golden striations. He looked a bit like Dwayne "The Rock" Johnson, only with hair and darker skin. Maxine believed The Rock was the sexiest man alive.

"Are you hurt?" He asked, those eyes full of concern. He sat up with her in his lap and for just a moment, Maxine forgot herself. Breathing became difficult. Then she felt something moist, clammy, and gooey down the length of her torso, and horror filled her.

Dennis hauled her to her feet, and Maxine came face to face with a man in chef's whites. Something dark and sweet-smelling covered him.

Maxine spotted the Queen's magnificent dress in a crumpled heap beneath her, splattered with the same substance dripping from her own clothing.

No! No, no, no.

Maxine shoved away from the man and grabbed the ruined dress. "Oh, my goodness. Look at this. Why didn't you watch where you were going?"

His face clouded. He gestured toward the constellation of broken dishes and overturned platters. "You crashed into me. Can't you just wipe it off?"

"This is chiffon! Can you just wipe off your—whatever the hell that was and serve it? It's ruined."

"I'm sure it can't be that bad. It's just a dress. Here—"

Maxine snatched it back out of his reach before he could touch it with his grubby mitts. "This is not some inconsequential frock. This is the Queen's swearing-in attire!" Her hard work had smeared remains of chocolate smashed on it. A flattened clump of the stuff peeled off and plopped to the floor at her feet. Maxine felt like crying.

She was a sticky mess, and the area around them was a disaster. Her mind was already whirling. They hadn't taken the shoes out yet; they were safe in their protective bag. There was chocolate splashed everywhere—on the furniture, the wall, and the jewelry. Even poor Dennis hadn't escaped. He had chocolate streaked across his glasses and his bald head.

She shook out the rumpled dress to assess the damage. Chocolate was ground into the fabric, and it was beyond repair. That much was clear. Maxine felt ill. Her dream—which had been so close only a moment ago—was over. Fury welled inside her until she was shaking with rage.

She turned her ire on the chef, who was muttering under his breath as he tried to clean up his broken dishes. Who was this careless guy, anyway?

Chapter Two

Nathan

NATHAN TUNED OUT THE woman's fussing, but when she spun away from him, he saw her skirt had hiked up, exposing a beautiful globe of ass. She looked to be wearing some minuscule pink thong, for heaven's sake. A petty part of him wanted to punish her for ruining his hard work, but decency and manners prevailed. He reached over and tugged her hem back into place.

She jerked and slapped his hand away with surprising force. "What the hell are you doing?"

"Your... ass was hanging out." Damn, she was prickly.

"Oh." She grumbled a thank you and returned to her lamentation.

Nathan squatted and went about gathering shards of broken crockery, his jaw clenched. There was nothing left of his masterpiece but hunks and crumbs. Yet *he* was at fault? She had some nerve to be bitching. "Give it a rest, lady. You're not the only one with a mess here."

"Is the world going to see your mess? Are they going to judge *your* mess on a world stage?"

When he looked up, Nathan had a moment's pause. She was practically breathing fire and covered with frosting. And why, for the love of everything, did she have to be quite pretty on top of all this aggravation? His body responded as though they were meeting for the first time at a casual event.

She may have had anger snapping in her eyes, but her skin was a smooth, rich dark brown. A riot of tawny, chin-length coils framed her high, broad cheekbones. He imagined the feel of them clutched in his fist as he lost himself inside those lush curves. A beauty mark near the corner of her mouth drew his attention. The downward tilt of her well-defined lips didn't detract from the sudden desire at all. The disaster forgotten for a moment, he imagined himself licking that chocolate right out of her abundant cleavage. *What the hell?*

Unsettled, Nathan snapped, "I think you might be blowing this out of proportion, don't you think?"

She jiggled the hanger in his direction and pinned him with an icy stare. "I've been working on this for weeks. How *dare—*"

The door to the Queen's office opened with a whoosh, and the woman herself stood there with a frown marring her pretty features. "What is happening out here?" She hissed. "The Prime Minister can hear you and I can't hear her." She caught sight of the utter devastation. It appeared as if there'd been an explosion in a bakery. "Oh, dear."

The Queen's majordomo, Joanne, hurried up the hallway, stepping over the mess in her kitten heels. She waved the Queen back into the office, assuring her she'd take care of this. Upon closing the door, she turned to Nathan and the cake destroyer and gasped.

"Is that—is that the Queen's luck cake? And her dress, as well?"

Nathan stood and tossed a handful of mess onto the table. That cloth would never be white again. "It *was*. Dammit."

Joanne looked at her dainty wristwatch, already in troubleshooting mode. "Alright, we have one hour and forty-five minutes before she's due at the High Court. Chef Nathan." Joanne's voice was so sharp it echoed and brought all the activity in the crowded hallway to a standstill. Nathan's spine stiffened. "You have a sous chef, correct?"

"Yes, of course."

"Can you make a new cake?"

"I can make *a* cake, not the luck cake. This took hours of—"

"Get on it and prepare something workable. Maxine!"

The woman jumped at the crack of Joanne's voice.

Nathan almost chuckled, despite himself. Joanne would have made an excellent teacher. Or a prison guard. Maybe even a battlefield commander. She'd run the previous Queen's affairs with military precision and continued to serve in her capacity in the new administration. The woman was just five feet, but she radiated gravitas and authority in her bearing. She exuded unruffled competence in a stylish pink pantsuit with her silver hair restrained in a no-nonsense bun.

So, the name of the klutz with the clothing rack of death was Maxine.

"You've prepared a host of outfits already for the Queen's upcoming engagements. Choose one to substitute."

Maxine gave a forlorn shake of her head. "Nothing is finished yet. She wasn't due for anything else official until late next week. We put all our efforts—*wait*. I believe I have something that will work. Dennis, what about the lodge dress?"

The young man that accompanied her paused in using his shirt hem to wipe ganache from his glasses. His owlish eyes brightened. "Yes! That could work. It needs—"

"The cuffs, I know. We could—"

They gathered up their cases, bags, and boxes with hasty motions. Then, with a desultory glance in his direction, Maxine the stylist swept out of the area with her assistant trailing in her wake. They were chattering a mile a minute.

Nathan ran through a mental checklist of remaining supplies for a replacement cake. There were still some fondant lace scrolls and extra gum paste flowers. He would be cutting it close, and the final product wouldn't be as elaborate as the original, but he could pull something together. The new Queen wouldn't know what to expect. Everything would be fine as long as they observed the tradition and sentiment.

Back in the kitchen, Nathan briefed his sous and head pastry chefs. Both women looked heartbroken but resolved. The three of them hammered out a plan and set about their tasks.

He popped the cake layers into the freezer to hasten their cooling and set a timer. While he waited, Nathan paused to survey his domain. What he saw pleased him. Close to 500 guests were expected for the feast banquet that evening, and the kitchen had been bustling for days in preparation. Like him, most of the staff had been there since four in the morning.

Whisking rum into the new batch of ganache, Nathan wished they'd decided on cake for the event's dessert. Then they could have just swapped out. No such luck, though—it was a buffet of bite-sized confections. Once he learned what the Queen's favorites were, he'd incorporate them into future menus. For now, the variety had seemed prudent. He'd ask another time.

Nathan could have handed the cake redux over, but he wasn't a bureaucrat who barked orders and then breathed down everyone's collective neck. It wasn't an effective management technique, and he abhorred leadership that wasn't willing to jump into the trenches.

The trenches were where Nathan had always thrived.

He set a new service tray on a rolling cart, then spun through the various stations to check in with his staff, tasting and adjusting seasonings here and there. Aside from the luck cake fiasco, things were rolling along almost perfectly.

Unbidden, Maxine's outraged expression came to mind as Nathan piped rosettes. Why the hell was she angry with him? It wasn't as though he'd singled her out and *thrown* the cake at her. She'd rallied, though.

Somehow, this cake surpassed the original. The tiers showcased different but complementary styles, representing the diversity of opinions the new monarch would face.

Nathan wiped sweat from his brow as he added the finishing touches, then stepped back to assess.

A glance at his watch showed he had all of eight minutes to get it upstairs in one piece. Hopefully, the comely Maxine wouldn't be anywhere in the vicinity. The Queen ought to be dressed by now.

Any other time, Nathan would just reverse the direction of the buttons on his double-breasted jacket, but no dice this time. He kept extras in his office for just such occasions. Nathan took a precious two minutes to clean himself up, then shrugged into a crisp, clean jacket. You never knew when you'd need to look sharp—a lesson learned from his mentor. A fresh toque, and he was ready.

Luck cake, take two.

Chapter Three

Maxine

BACK IN HER STUDIO after a harrowing trip across town, Maxine hung up the unfinished dress and studied it with Dennis. They'd designed this dress for a reception with the judges of the High Court and it was a bit more conservative than their original choice. While the hemline needed adjusting and the cuffs could use some embellishment, she could make this work.

Maxine had planned jewel tones to complement the Queen's complexion and personality, but perhaps this more muted palette would better suit the somber occasion. A splash of color with the shoes, sassy jewelry, and that confidence and earnestness that had gotten her elected as monarch. That should do the trick.

"Okay, let's get to work."

"Uh, boss?" Dennis gestured at her front. "You're still wearing cake."

An impatient huff escaped her pursed lips when Maxine glanced down at her dress. It was one of her favorites, now possibly ruined. She'd attempt to salvage it later. "Get started," she instructed. "I'll be right back."

The studio had once been a textile factory, and Maxine kept a futon in her small office for when she worked late and didn't feel up to making the hour-long drive home. A quick shower cleared her mind, even though she kept picturing a pair of golden-brown eyes filled with annoyance.

With her thoughts less jumbled and her mood improved, Maxine chided herself for her earlier behavior. She'd had a full-on tantrum, whereas the chef's concern had been a possible injury. A twinge of guilt zinged through her. *Damn.*

She might owe him an apology. She'd think about it more when this ordeal was over.

Damn that man, and damn his cake, too.

By the time she stepped back from the dress form, Maxine's hands, shoulders, and back were aching.

"Let's pack it up."

Almost two hours after the disaster, the Queen was none the wiser as she dressed in a chic ensemble of camel and black with red pumps. A blend of modern and traditional styles, it honored her island heritage.

Maxine breathed a sigh of relief once she stood back to examine her handiwork. Made up and with her braids pinned into an intricate updo for when the crown was placed upon her head, the Queen was resplendent. Just 26, she was the youngest Queen in Lytua's history—nearly young enough to be Maxine's daughter.

Maxine's heart was hammering. She wasn't sure whose approval she needed most, but both the Queen and Joanne seemed pleased. The Queen even praised the surprise switch—since Maxine had unveiled a different dress a few days before. That dress was now in the rubbish bin, but Maxine kept silent about that. Perhaps she'd recreate the ruined dress another time.

"There you are, my Queen. Just lovely." Maxine had never felt such pride surging through her at one of her creations.

The young woman beamed at her, but nerves tinged her smile. "I'm not officially the Queen until after I take my oath and choose my ceremonial name."

"Which one did you decide on?" Joanne asked.

The Queen's smile grew even wider. "You'll find out with everyone else when I tell the story."

After a brisk knock, the chef breezed into the office and presented a gorgeous confection with a flourish. He gave Maxine a wide berth and a little side-eye. Maxine managed to keep from snarling. She shoved her annoyance back down. This wasn't the time or place.

The assembled group oohed and aahed appropriately.

"Nothing as beautiful as our new Queen, but merely a humble offering." The chef's voice was silky, damn near flirtatious. Nothing like earlier when he'd spoken to her. He even gave an ostentatious bow that made her roll her eyes. Maxine's irritation with the man grew, then she chastised herself. Why was she concerned if he was flirting with the Queen?

The Queen blushed and looked so very young at that moment, with tentative eagerness in her eyes instead of shadows.

Maxine had only seen the broken remnants of the first cake, but even her untrained eye could appreciate the intricate decorations.

"It's almost too pretty to eat," Joanne cooed, and Maxine had to agree.

Using a pearl-handled server, the chef cut into the cake, and the deft movements of his hand mesmerized Maxine. He recounted the legend of the luck cake as he sliced and plated it.

"The customary luck cake is a tradition dating back to our island's founding. The incoming ruler was to enjoy a symbolic helping right before being crowned. It represents the peace and prosperity the Kingdom hopes to experience with a new leader. A reminder to stay grounded and humble and true to the people. No matter the title, the new monarch is still merely a man or woman who eats one bite at a time, just like everyone else."

Lytuans could be a superstitious lot, but there was no fault to be found here.

The chef served the cake to everyone in the office, and their fingers brushed when Maxine accepted her slice. It felt like an electric shock went through her.

Her gaze flew to his face, but he wasn't looking at her, having moved on to the next person.

"To a sweet reign," he offered, holding his plate aloft.

"A sweet reign," Maxine echoed with the others and took a nibble. Flavor exploded on her tongue, and she took a larger bite. Everyone was making noises of delight, their faces lighting up with joy. *Oh, dear Lord.* Maxine thought it tasted like how an orgasm felt. Mind-blowing and utterly decadent, like sorcery. She closed her eyes to savor it properly. She'd never tasted anything more divine, and she didn't even much *care* for cake. The man was a master.

She found the chef watching her with interest alight in his unusual eyes. The smallest, self-satisfied smile quirked up one corner of his mouth. Her face grew hot, and her heart thumped hard. She turned away from that too-knowing gaze, wondering why she felt suddenly breathless. If she didn't know better…!

He was looking at her like he wanted to smear that exquisite frosting on her somewhere naughty and lick it off. His bold perusal hinted at that innate, particular swagger that men well over six feet seemed to have. He was good-looking and knew it. Maxine downed her glass of champagne and refused to think about that chiseled jaw or those enviably thick and lustrous eyebrows.

Her work here was done, and now she could go and celebrate with the other citizens. She'd narrowly avoided getting sacked. She would not let that arrogant chef know he'd gotten to her.

Certainly not.

Chapter Four

Nathan

Two Years Later

T HE QUEEN'S FLAG WASN'T flying over the Hubbard Building—affectionately known as the Hub by locals—which meant she was off-island. The place was likely a ghost town. Nathan himself was supposed to be in Costa Rica on a much-needed vacation with his daughter and son-in-law, but during brunch just two days ago, she'd announced she was pregnant. Flying in the early stages wasn't a good idea. They'd have to reschedule.

Nathan liked *The Kid* well enough, but the reality of the guy knocking up his baby girl activated something visceral. Nathan stalled before Ericka could read too much into his stunned silence in the wake of her bombshell. He shoveled a forkful of roast into his mouth to give his brain a chance to work. The impulse to snatch The Kid up by his scrawny neck and shake him receded as he chewed, and by the time he'd swallowed, he could offer sincere congratulations.

Nathan grimaced as he pulled into his assigned parking space in the underground garage. With his schedule clear for two weeks, he'd been at loose ends that morning and thought to occupy himself with work. He took the stairs to the second floor, where his office and the commercial kitchen were located. As predicted, no one was there.

He donned his work apron, even though he wouldn't be cooking today. Old habits. Another old habit had him casting a critical eye around the empty kitchen. Everything was sparkling and seemed in order. *Excellent.* He ran his kitchen with ruthless efficiency and didn't tolerate sloppiness.

Managing a staff of thirty felt like being the mayor of a small city at times, but he had talented leadership in place. Things ran like a well-oiled machine most of the time. The last year had been hell, though, with his sous chef on parental leave. She was still finding her footing after returning a few weeks ago. Nathan didn't doubt she'd find her way but made a mental note to schedule a one-on-one with her to check in.

Nathan compared the large dry-erase wall calendar to his personal calendar of events. Things were on track to welcome the interns from the high school magnet culinary program next month. A spate of seasonal events was on the horizon, including his favorite—the showcase where university students created fine dining out of traditional dorm food. He absorbed himself in some menu planning work. Anything to keep from thinking about how he was going to be a granddad at the ripe old age of forty-six.

He and his ex-wife had gotten married right out of college and had Ericka the following year. To his initial dismay, Ericka had followed in their footsteps and married young at 20 before finishing her university studies. The shock of their elopement had hit hard. Once Nathan had calmed down, he'd been adamant that she finish her degree. No child of his would depend entirely on their spouse for finances or anything else. They'd lived with him for the first two years of their marriage to save money to buy their own place. Nathan was rattling around in his empty house without them. The thought of downsizing had seemed attractive. But now that a new grandbaby was coming? *Not so much.*

He couldn't be prouder of his brilliant girl, who was working on her doctorate in chemical engineering. The Kid was head over heels in love and doted on her. He'd give him that. He had a backbone and had stood his ground against Nathan on multiple occasions. Ericka wasn't his little girl in pigtails with a gap-toothed grin anymore. She was someone's wife and about to be a mother. Thinking about that gave him a bittersweet ache in his chest.

Nathan brewed a cappuccino and enjoyed it while standing at one of the large islands in the workspace. Normally, there was a beehive of activity in this cavernous room. The constant clatter of plates and shouted directions—Nathan thrived on those, but he could appreciate this quiet stillness, too. He needed to hear what was happening in the kitchen and had refused soundproofing for his office. When he needed quiet, he sought it elsewhere. His previous life didn't require silence like this. Now he needed it to give the demons time to loosen their choke hold on his sanity and let him breathe.

Before being hired as the executive chef five years ago, he'd eaten in the employee cafeteria only a handful of times—always with his brothers and sisters of the Queen's Elite Guard. The familiar twinge of guilt when he thought of how his time with them had ended almost derailed him. Nathan immediately slammed the door on that memory and distracted himself by scrolling through the newspaper headlines on his phone.

He skimmed an article on the Queen's recent remarks on infrastructure improvement plans. He didn't agree with all her decisions but respected how hands-on and hardworking she was. Her enthusiasm had held so far, and she'd established herself as the people's Queen straightaway.

"Huh," Nathan harrumphed when he read the short mention of how Maxine Abernathy would redesign the postal carriers' uniforms. Ever since their disastrous meeting over their destroyed masterpieces years before, he and Maxine hadn't interacted often, but it was always tense and uncomfortable when they did. They even avoided each other at staff events. Nathan and the Queen's stylist were like oil and water. One professional to another, though, he admired her work from afar. The Queen always looked great.

Maxine herself was a knockout—voluptuous and sultry, with the sexy confidence that came from living your best life without apology. Classy and stylish, she was following her dreams, and it looked good as hell on her. Too bad she ruined it every time she opened her mouth. Her tongue cut like a blade. She seemed to hold him in particular contempt, and it rankled.

Best to put her out of his mind.

A glance at his watch convinced Nathan he'd done enough for the day. He washed and dried his cup and saucer, whistling as he cleaned the espresso machine. He'd made sufficient progress on event plans to be satisfied for now. After typing a summary memo, he took the elevator to the Queen's office.

He held his badge up to the reader next to the door, then pressed his palm to the glass screen. The comforting beep confirming his access sounded right away. The eerie quiet followed him up. Everyone must be knocking off since the Queen was off-island.

He'd just leave the folder with the updates in the inbox atop her desk. He smiled to himself. The Queen did not like to have others sort her tasks or filter information for her. She was insistent about removing gatekeepers. Nathan liked that about her and knew she'd want to meet once she'd reviewed his memo.

As he was about to leave, Nathan stopped to scribble a thought on one of the proposed menus. He glanced up when the office door whooshed open, and a clothing rack full of hanging garment bags rolled in at speed, pushed by none other than Maxine, the resident cake destroyer. As though he'd conjured her.

Nathan's jaw clenched, and he tucked the pencil behind his ear. She might seem to detest him, but she was alluring as hell with that hourglass figure. Today she was wearing a lightweight jersey dress, waist cinched in with a wide belt.

The pleasant expression on her face soured when she caught sight of him. The rack slowed to a stop as the door closed behind her. "Chef." She looked at him like something she'd scraped off the bottom of those stilettos she wore.

"Maxine." Did she even know his name? He couldn't recall her ever using it.

"I'll come back later."

"Don't let me run you out of here. I'm just about done."

"You're not harboring any flying cakes, are you?"

Nathan's eyebrows shot up. "Am I imagining things or are you making a joke?" He didn't know what to think.

"I've been known to occasionally."

"You always seem so uptight, taking your work so seriously."

"I'm not uptight."

She had obviously heard the accusation before, as her clapback was so swift. Nathan regretted the impulsive description. "I'm just dropping off."

"Me, too."

He watched out of the corner of his eye as she started transferring the garment bags to a closet on the far side of the office. Nathan studied the notes he'd just made, rethinking them.

"What brings the mighty chef to the Hub on a quiet day like today?" Her voice carried a subtle note of... disdain.

"Same as you—duty." Nathan forced his shoulders to relax. "Revisions to the menu for the garden party."

"The one for the aunties and grandmothers? I'm planning a gorgeous polka-dot fit and flare for her."

"Florals too mundane?" He managed to stay light on the sarcasm. Progress.

"Far too common. She'll make a bold statement more suited to her personality. I'm sure you prefer the unexpected, too. I bet there won't be a cucumber finger sandwich in sight."

Nathan snorted. "Over my dead body."

Okay, so maybe he'd been a bit of a dick after *the incident.* He'd been beyond annoyed about his own ruined creation and not very understanding about hers.

While they had argued, he'd had the most inopportune image of himself licking the frosting from where it had been all in her cleavage. He'd never been able to shake that image.

That nasty run-in had set the tone for all their subsequent interactions. She wandered uninvited into his thoughts every so often, sometimes his dreams. He did his best to steer clear of her in his waking hours. Nathan tried to concentrate on the notes he wanted to write but couldn't remember a damn thing. *Curse that woman.* He could smell her perfume. Something straight-up sexy that was more tantalizing than it should be. It was spicy and magnetic and tugging at him.

Everything about her bothered him, and he was sure it was entirely mutual. However, there was no reason he couldn't still enjoy looking at her, and there was plenty to enjoy. He'd never admit to fantasizing about her curvy little body intertwined with his. It was childish of him to antagonize her when he could tell he flustered her.

What he should do was get the hell out of there before they started bickering again. But Nathan hesitated and couldn't explain why.

Chapter Five

MAXINE HOISTED TWO MORE bags from the garment rack and headed to the closet, turning her back to the hot chef. She steadied her shaking hands through sheer force of will.

When she'd caught sight of him standing by the Queen's desk, there'd been a split-second where she wanted to execute an immediate about-face, drop everything, then run like hell. She'd harbored something of a secret crush on the man since the day their worlds collided two years ago. Not that she'd ever tell him that. It was so much easier to try to ignore him.

But Chef Nathan Olivier was not the kind of man you ignored.

Instead of his usual kitchen attire, he was dressed in well-worn jeans and a fitted soft-looking heathered tee that clung to him and highlighted all his assets. He was working some impressive biceps and pecs. He'd appeared shirtless on the cover of last month's edition of *Lytua Week* with a gleaming cleaver resting against his shoulder like a machete, unfastened jeans slung low on a narrow waist. The smoldering look he was giving the camera was enough to set the capital city of Augustus atwitter. He was the fittest chef she'd ever seen, that was for sure. She'd spent far too long staring at those powerful-looking shoulders and sculpted abs. He was even hotter up close, which Maxine found vaguely offensive for reasons she didn't want to examine. That didn't mean she couldn't admire the view, though. It wasn't exactly a hardship.

He was older than her, with one of those timeless faces that made an accurate guess on age impossible. According to the article, though, he was eight years her senior. The gray threading his temples and short locs lent an air of distinction, and then there were those golden-brown eyes. Maxine had to suppress a shiver.

He was cocky, but she kind of liked it on him. Not that she'd ever tell him that, either.

Why was she always attracted to unsuitable men? Her track record of late was full of decent first dates but few second ones. Maxine scoffed. What did it matter? She wasn't looking for love. She'd been down that road before, and it had led her straight to extended heartache.

When Maxine snuck a glance at Nathan, her pulse leaped, and she nearly bobbled the bag she was holding. He was watching her.

"So, what do you have there?" He waved a hand at the garment rack. Even his voice was sexy—curse him.

"Wardrobing for the Queen's trip next week. We're going to Quebec. Thanks to you, everything is now sealed and disaster-proof. Nothing gets unwrapped until we're safe behind a closed door."

"Interesting. How do you keep track of what's what, then?"

She lifted a bag off the rack and turned it towards him. "We catalog everything. We number and date them, put care info and a picture of the completed outfit inside, and there's a small window here on the shoulder."

"That's an efficient system."

"I'm not uptight," she reiterated, her cheeks feeling hot.

"No, that was a genuine compliment." He wandered over for a closer look. Maxine had to remind herself to breathe and act naturally. "You've included a notes section, too. I'm assuming for after she's worn it? That's brilliant."

Maxine had to clear her throat and steel herself against the pleasure that bloomed within her at his unexpected words. With him standing close, she caught his zesty, refreshing scent. It was light and salty, conjuring images of the beach after a fast-moving rainstorm. *Yum.* "Yes—for things you may not think about again once you've taken it off. Like the hem kept riding up or the skirt fabric was itchy. Joanne has an eagle eye for detail. The feedback helps me to improve." *Oh, God*, she willed herself to stop babbling. "Ah, if you'll excuse me, I need to—"

"Of course. I didn't mean to waylay you."

Great. So he was gracious on top of charming. He was already starring in late-night fantasies she'd die before admitting to. Lord, it just wasn't fair.

Nathan Olivier would have been completely insufferable if he wasn't so damn good at what he did.

Despite her nerves jangling, Maxine remained placid on the outside as she returned to her task of arranging the Queen's clothing. She watched him on the sly, hoping she was being surreptitious about it.

She'd heard the rumors about him but had never considered whether they were true. He had a reputation for being the love 'em and leave 'em type. Her mind strayed, wondering if the loving might be well worth the price of the leaving.

Maxine fumbled an accessories pouch but was able to snag it before it hit the floor.

Concentrate, Maxine!

Maxine was too skittish to eat in the staff cafeteria. Before she knew differently, she'd reasoned that running into him there would be a stretch. He wasn't a line cook—he wasn't likely to be serving the actual food. Sure enough, though, he was often found doing just that, even when it wasn't a special occasion. That first time she'd stepped inside and seen him at the carving station in his pristine chef's whites, her heart tripped, and she was tempted to skip lunch altogether. The smells had been divine, though, and she'd be damned if she let him stop her from a heavenly meal. He'd disappeared by the time she'd meandered her way to his station, and Maxine wasn't altogether sure if she was disappointed or relieved.

Maxine cursed when she realized she'd gotten distracted and mixed up the order of the bags.

"You okay?" he called.

"Fine," she snapped and wished she didn't sound so perturbed. Didn't he say he was finishing up? Perhaps she should hide in the closet until he left? She shook her head, disgusted with herself for even entertaining the ludicrous thought.

When her mobile rang with the cheery ringtone she'd assigned to Dennis, Maxine smiled and fished it out of her pocket. "Stop freaking out," she admonished by way of greeting. "It's going to be wonderful."

Dennis' frantic voice rose over the thumping bass of a club beat in the background. "I'm not ready! I'm calling the whole thing off!"

"You're not calling off your first solo fashion show. Dennis, you've got this."

"Max, I'm going to puke."

A sound from the other room reminded her of Nathan's presence. Maxine sat down on the floor with the phone cradled to her ear and pulled the closet door closed some. "To be honest, I'd be worried if you weren't nervous. You're ready and it's going to be spectacular. No one will know about any mishaps unless you tell them. You're the expert here."

Dennis let out a shaky sigh. "And you're sure you can't make it? I could use some of your Zen right now."

"I'm so sorry, but this conference was planned over a year ago. There was just no way I could get out of it. You'll do great, I know it."

What her faithful assistant didn't know was that she'd rescheduled so that she could be there to surprise him. She'd been conspiring with his mother and boyfriend for months.

By the time they hung up, Dennis had stopped panicking and was back to his levelheaded, pragmatic self. Maxine couldn't help but smile as she fired off a quick text to his boyfriend and then a longer one to his mother, confirming that the surprise was still on. She'd wrap things up here, scoot by the chef, and get on with her plan.

An alarm sounded a few minutes later, making Maxine jump and straighten from where she'd been crouched organizing bags of shoes. Klaxons were blaring.

There was an announcement that a test would commence in ten seconds and that all personnel should be clear. Then the alarm went silent.

Puzzled, she poked her head out of the closet just in time to hear the *snick* of electronic locks engaging. The chef stood next to the Queen's desk, looking as confused as she felt. Maxine strode to the door and tugged on the handle, but it remained firmly closed. "It's locked."

"Surely not."

"You're welcome to try."

Nathan placed his folder on the Queen's desk and tried the door. When it didn't budge, he tried the other one. It, too, held fast. "What the hell?"

Maxine tamped down the urge to say *I told you so,* because nothing good ever came of that. If she'd learned only one thing from her marriage unraveling, it was that. Regret was like a spear in her belly. "I can't be locked in here. I have places to be."

"Right. You're the type who puts your own selfish interests ahead of their mentee's."

Maxine rounded on him. "What does that mean?"

"Seems like you could have been there for his big night, don't you think?"

Heat flooded her face. She glared up at him. "You were eavesdropping on me?" The cheek on him!

"You were talking loudly," he shot back. "I'd never leave my mentee to fly solo like that."

Her back up now, Maxine sniffed. "Not that it's any of your business, but I made arrangements with his mother to surprise him. He only *thinks* I won't be there."

"Oh." All his righteous indignation deflated. *Score one for me.* "Well, that's quite lovely, then, isn't it?"

"Shall we work on getting out of here now, or would you prefer to pick apart more of my life choices?"

He had the decency to look chagrined.

The main office doors were locked, but another closet, a small storage room, and the Queen's private bathroom remained open.

Frowning, Nathan put his hands on his hips. Maxine tried not to ogle his rippling biceps. "I heard an announcement earlier but didn't pay much attention. They're always having drills."

"Do you know what they're testing?" Maxine asked, but when Nathan shook his head, she stuffed down a rising sense of panic. "Okay, time to call Jaden, then."

"*Jaden*?" Nathan crowed with a smirk. "You're on a first-name basis with the Captain of the Queen's Elite Guard?"

Maxine dug out her phone and flushed as she thought of the very tall, very muscular, very *intense* Jaden Everly, with his deep voice and penetrating gaze. Whew, the way that man exuded raw masculinity left most women quivering from a simple hello. She wasn't immune. "He's gorgeous, yes," she admitted. "But he's also a happy newlywed. I don't poach or date where I work." Maxine hoped Jaden's new wife was a very contented woman indeed. It would be a damn waste otherwise. *Good for her.*

After unlocking her screen, Maxine saw that her last text—the one to Dennis' mother—showed as "failed". How peculiar. The Hub had excellent reception. She scrolled through her contacts list but only heard dead air when she tried to dial Jaden. "It won't connect."

Nathan, too, seemed to have Jaden on speed dial, but the result was the same when he called. "I can't get a signal."

"What would disable the electronics?" Maxine picked up the desk line from the side table. It was dead. "Nothing."

Nathan searched the pad calendar on Joanne's desk in the far corner of the room. "Uh-oh."

Her stomach took a nosedive. Maxine replaced the receiver on its cradle and turned to him. "That sounds ominous. What's up?"

"It says 'New System Lockdown Test, remote'."

"Ah. That shouldn't take long." Maxine plopped down into a wing chair and crossed her legs, resigned to the temporary delay.

"We're going to be waiting a while. This shows the next two days blocked off."

Maxine rocketed to her feet in outrage. *"What?* I can't stay here for two days!"

"The notes say lockdown, so nothing in or out."

"We're really stuck here? Together? For two days?"

"Looks like it."

"Oh, no, Dennis' show! I need to get in touch with the rest of my team. We have an event tomorrow night."

"Can they handle it?"

"They'll have to. But they'll be worried."

"Maybe they won't even notice you're gone."

Was he teasing her? She could never tell. "Maybe your staff wouldn't notice, but mine will. What are you doing?"

The infuriating man was peering up into the ceiling corners.

"What are you looking for?"

"The cameras we can signal."

Maxine shook her head. "There are no cameras in this room."

"Yes there are, when—"

His contradiction grated on her nerves. He was such a know-it-all. "The Queen removed them."

"Crap. What about the panic buttons?" He reached under the desk. "It triggers a silent alarm, but unless the cavalry comes busting in, we can assume those are deactivated, as well. The Queen's on the other side of the world right now. I bet Jaden knows what's up."

Maxine made a face at him. There was a subtle note of mockery in his voice when he said Jaden's name. Oh, what had she gotten herself into now?

Chapter Six

NATHAN

He couldn't seem to stop himself from provoking her. Why did her mention of Jaden's good looks cause something like a fine thread of jealousy to ripple through him? Nathan frowned as he leaned a hip against Joanne's desk and crossed his ankles.

He knew Jaden, of course. They'd been close colleagues during the previous Queen's reign. Right up until—*no*. He would not think about that today.

Maxine started pacing, wringing her hands. "So, what do we do?"

"What *can* we do? This entire office is a panic room. We're not going anywhere. This would explain why it's a ghost town. Were you supposed to be here today?"

A scowl crossed her face. "No. I just had a pocket of time."

"Same here. My vacation plans got canceled at the last minute. Okay, let's take stock. This could be exponentially worse." Even as he started problem-solving, he was determined to put a positive spin on things. Another old quirk cropping up.

She stopped pacing long enough to shoot him a glare. *"How?"*

"We could have no bathroom or no water. Or no electricity."

Maxine gasped. "Why would you put that out there into the universe? That's just tempting—"

At that exact moment, the electricity shut off. The lights winked out and the air conditioning fell silent. Maxine closed her eyes and looked to be holding on to her patience with both hands. Her lips were moving, perhaps in silent prayer.

Her eyes held fire when she opened them again. "It's ninety-eight degrees outside. We'll cook!"

"We won't. The sun will go down soon, and it'll cool off."

Maxine rushed to the windows and threw the curtains back. "There's no opening mechanism. It's going to be a swamp in here tomorrow. I can't believe this is happening."

"There are worse things, I'm sure."

"You underestimate how annoying you are."

Ouch. There was nothing for him to say to that. She didn't like him at all. In fact, she looked like she wanted to wring his neck. She resumed her pacing while Nathan considered their next steps.

She huffed out a breath. "Maybe we should break a window?"

"Can't. They're bulletproof."

She paused her pacing and whirled to face him. "How are you so calm? This is spiking my anxiety. What are we going to do for two days? Where will we sleep? What about food? I'm already getting hangry."

They both looked over at the sofa, an unassuming modern design in vivid turquoise fabric. Maxine's distress was palpable. "It's big enough for both of us, I think. We'll figure it out later. I can help solve the hangry part right now, though." Nathan retrieved his emergency snack from the apron he still wore. "I've got a slightly smashed protein bar. Take it."

She eyed it the way you would a venomous snake.

"It's not a marriage proposal, Maxine. Take it and eat."

"But what will you eat?"

"I'm okay for now. And I think you need it more than I do."

The desire to refuse was there in her eyes, but hunger won out. She accepted it and ripped the wrapper open. "Thank you."

She wolfed it down in four bites and licked chocolate from her thumb. The sight of her tongue riveted Nathan. His cock throbbed. *Oh, hell.*

"How do you know so much about the Queen's office?" She asked. And her voice held a slight accusatory note.

"I've been around a while."

Nathan didn't wait to see what she thought of his vague explanation. He turned his back to her and tugged the curtains closed. They were insubstantial sheers but would block at least some of the heat. "It's a full moon tonight, so that will provide some light." She was staring at him. "What?"

"I get the sense there's more to you than meets the eye."

His heart hammered hard. There used to be. "Nope. What you see is what you get, Madam Stylist."

Maxine grumbled as she looked around. She stepped out of her heels and tucked them under the sofa, out of the way. She unfastened her belt and tossed it into a chair. When she billowed the neckline of her dress back and forth to get some air, Nathan forced himself to look away.

"We're going to be here for a while, so I vote we call a truce. Bickering and sniping don't do us any good."

"Truce, then," she agreed.

"Let's scope out whatever we can find before it gets dark. You look in that closet, and I'll look in this one. Bring out anything interesting and put it on the table there. We'll see what we've got and make a plan from there."

Confusion zipped through Nathan when she didn't move. "Maxine? Did you hear me?"

"Oh, I heard you." She crossed her arms, looking mutinous.

"Then what's wrong?"

"You toss out orders and expect them to be obeyed. I'm sure that works well for you in your domain, but this isn't your kitchen, and I don't work for you."

Now why the hell did that make his dick hard? Nathan gritted his teeth. "Fair enough. I'll try to ask a little more... politely." She was more receptive when he rephrased.

She disappeared into one closet, and he turned his attention to the other. It was something of a butler's pantry in the storage closet, but no luck. It was only stocked with two small packets of nuts and pretzels. Both were almost a decade out of date and sure to be a straight shot to food poisoning. Nathan made a sound of disgust and chucked them into the trash bin.

He didn't want to admit it, but it was already getting stuffy in the airless room. Sweat trickled down between his shoulder blades.

Their foraging turned up a few comestibles—assorted condiment packets, a single bottle of water, and an ancient can of pears, of all things.

"Great," Maxine lamented as they surveyed their meager bounty. "A chef of your caliber can whip something up out of this disparate stuff, right?"

"No sweat."

"Truly?"

"Of course not. I'm not a magician."

An honest-to-God giggle escaped her. Maxine clapped a hand over her mouth to stifle it.

It was so cute Nathan laughed himself. "Well, there's only one other place to look."

When she saw where he was pointing, it appalled Maxine. "We're not rifling through the Queen's desk!"

"She wouldn't want us to starve, now, would she?"

Maxine sighed. "Maybe she keeps a stash of chocolate in there somewhere."

They didn't find any chocolate, but Nathan wasn't bothered. A couple of days without eating wouldn't do any permanent damage. He'd gone longer than that on training maneuvers, but he was wise enough to keep that sentiment to himself. "Let's look again, this time for anything useful."

He was sifting through the items under the bathroom sink when a muffled clatter and expletive floated out from the closet where Maxine was foraging. When he went to investigate, he couldn't believe his eyes. She was balanced precariously on her toes at the top of a three-rung stepstool and was about to break her neck reaching for something far back on the top shelf.

"What the hell are you doing?" He boomed at her.

With a startled yelp, Maxine toppled from the stepstool, but Nathan caught her up against him. He got a face full of sweet-smelling softness and his hands beneath an ass that felt better than it should have.

She pushed back from his chest to look down at him with wide eyes as she dangled in his arms. "Wow, that was close. You have excellent reflexes. Thank you."

"Do you have a death wish? Why didn't you ask me to get it for you?"

Ignoring him, she made an impatient gesture with her hand. "Here, help me to the top shelf. I think there's a bottle of wine back there."

Rather than boost her up, Nathan set her down on her bare feet. Maybe a little more forcefully than he'd intended. She wore silver rings around several of her perfectly pedicured, magenta-painted toes. Nathan grunted in exasperation. Why the hell would he notice something like that?

"Back up," he barked. When she flinched, he mumbled, "Sorry." She stepped away to give him room.

He pulled down an old file box with faded lettering on the side and sat it on a side table. "See what's in that."

When Maxine merely raised an eyebrow at him, Nathan expelled a sigh, then gritted his teeth and amended, "Please."

The stepstool gave him the extra height he needed to snag the neck of the dusty, unlabeled bottle. He took it to where Maxine was busy rummaging through the contents of the storage box. "Looks like we found someone's stash of hooch."

Maxine looked hopeful, then she frowned as a thought occurred to her. "We don't have a wine opener, though. Damn."

Nathan held up a finger, then fished around in his apron to bring up a little corkscrew bottle opener. He jiggled it at her.

She peered at the fabric tied to his waist. "What else do you have in there?"

"Now that's a loaded question, isn't it, love?"

She laughed again and damned if he didn't like that sound. "You are a hopeless flirt."

"Nobody would accuse me of otherwise. Let's break this open." Nathan set about opening the dark bottle of mystery booze and pointed at the box with his chin. "What'd you find?"

"You'll love it, but let's have some wine first."

Nathan gave the contents of the bottle a sniff and flashed her a grin. "Not wine. Smells like someone's homemade guava berry rum."

"Ooh, even better."

The way she lit up with that pretty mouth rounded into a perfect "o" made blood rush to Nathan's lower half. It heightened his awareness of her unpleasantly. "We don't have any cups or glasses, so you first."

"I'm not going to argue."

He couldn't take his eyes off how the rum dribbled down her chin and neck when she drank from the bottle. Laughing, she wiped it away with the back of her hand. The amber liquid collected in the collar of her dress and modest cleavage. Jesus, Nathan wanted nothing more than to hook a finger into her neckline and tug so he could lick and suck that sticky sweetness from the smooth skin between her breasts. Then up that long, graceful neck of hers to—

"Chef?"

Nathan snapped his attention back. What the hell was going on with him? He was acting like a horny teenager. "It's hot, and we're likely dehydrated. Take this slow or we'll be shitfaced in a blink."

The speculative look she gave him spoke volumes. "Were you a scout?"

"No. What makes you ask?"

"You're so watchful, so... levelheaded and responsible. Like everything is a puzzle to be figured out."

Nathan grunted in response. He wasn't feeling particularly levelheaded or responsible right now. What he was feeling was good old-fashioned lust.

For a woman who couldn't stand him.

God help him, it was going to be a long two days.

Chapter Seven

WITH THE PLEASANT RUM buzz taking the edge off the heat, Maxine said, "You'll never guess what's in the box." She reached in and produced a deck of cards.

Nathan squinted at the title, then gave her a heart-stopping grin. "Truth or dare? Seriously? What's that doing here?"

"No idea, but it takes care of entertainment. I don't think the Queen is the type to hide rum and a children's card game."

"I agree. Maybe it's the naughty version."

"Maybe the previous Queen was kinkier than any of us knew?"

"Or maybe the current Queen is. You never know. Kinky people are everywhere."

"True." Maxine pictured the staid, almost dour previous Queen. They both broke out laughing. "No way."

"We'll come back to the entertainment. Next issue—sleeping arrangements." They turned to contemplate the sofa. It was a lovely piece of furniture with heavy suede fabric decorated with a multitude of throw pillows. "At least it has a lot of pillows. It'll be cooler on the floor."

They worked together to arrange a nest of sorts. When she gave it a skeptical look, he reassured her. "It'll be fine. We'll deal with it later. I'm curious about the other contents of that box."

Besides the truth or dare deck, they found a conversation guide for first dates and a similar board game. "What in the world was somebody getting up to in here? I hope they cleaned the upholstery before the Queen took her oath."

His laugh was low and deep, triggering a quiver somewhere deep inside Maxine. Watching the strong column of his throat work as he drank the rum was enthralling. She tried not to stare or contemplate how potent her desire was to brush her lips there. Imagining the pleasured sounds he'd make if she did had her temperature rising once more. Somehow, Maxine resisted the urge to fan herself and grabbed the truth or dare cards instead. She retreated to one of the side chairs and resisted the urge to look as Nathan toed off his loafers and nudged them under the sofa.

She snuck a glance at his feet when he crossed them in front of her, half hoping they were ashy and busted so she could freeze this attraction. No such luck. Of *course,* his feet were meticulously cared for—no ragged claws or ash to be found. Damn. That would have been an easy deal breaker. She loved it when men leveled up their grooming habits. Did he get regular pedicures? How the hell was she finding his feet attractive?

Forcing her gaze away from his toes and to the game, Maxine fidgeted with the edges of the cards. They both had a few more sips of rum, taking turns. The tang burned her throat a little every time, and she wished she had some juice or ginger ale to cut it.

"Let me guess," Nathan ventured. "You'd prefer this with a mixer?"

Holy hell. It was like he'd read her mind. "How did you…?"

"You make a face every time you swallow."

A zip of fear flitted through Maxine's belly. She'd been told her entire life that she had an expressive face. She stunk at poker. If she wasn't careful, the hot chef would catch onto the fact that she was lusting after him.

And she couldn't have that. No way in hell.

Chapter Eight

Nathan

S HE WASN'T HIS TYPE, Nathan reminded himself. Far too contrary. She'd be good for a tumble and maybe a weekend, but otherwise, she was too much work. Nathan liked his women agreeable and enthusiastic. There would be nothing easy in dealing with Maxine Abernathy. His libido had a very different assessment, though. Part of him wondered if she might be worth the hassle.

Why the hell was he thinking of the cake destroyer romantically at a time like this?

Don't go there, Nathan.

Nathan untied and removed his apron, folded it, and placed it on a side table. The stale, hot air was uncomfortably warm, and while his T-shirt was sticking to him, she looked like a wilted flower sitting there. She ran the back of her wrist over her brow to wipe off the sweat. Hell, there were much, much better ways for them to get sweaty together.

Not supposed to be going there. Nathan blurted out the first thing that came to mind. "This could be the plot of a cheesy romance novel, don't you think? A couple of sworn enemies trapped together and forced to depend on one another in extreme circumstances."

When she said nothing, he doubled down and added the most outlandish things he could think of. He wanted to take her mind off the heat.

"Throw in some improbable dialog, a few references to tumescent manhood, a fake engagement, and all that jazz. Bonus points for a secluded snowy mountaintop cabin with only one bed where they need to keep each other warm."

The corner of Maxine's mouth twitched, and she bit her lip. "How do you know all these tropes?"

"I may or may not have read too many of my older sister's romance novels at an impressionable age. The only thing missing from this scenario is a secret baby. Maybe a billionaire or a down-on-his-luck duke."

She snickered. "Do you take anything seriously?"

Nathan sobered, his memory flashing to the anguish on his friend's face. He shoved that gut-wrenching image down as deep as it would go, even as his jaw clenched. Usually, he kept a better lock on that. Turning away from her, he was careful to keep his voice neutral. "Serious is overrated."

Boredom took hold as the room grew ever stuffier. They shared the pears, careful not to cut their fingers as they scooped them out through the can's pull-tab style opening. Nathan convinced himself he wasn't interested in how she slurped the fruit and its juices. Nor curious about how she might respond to him using his tongue to help her with the stickiness.

"What would you be doing if you weren't here?" Her question interrupted his thoughts from lapsing further into the gutter.

"Most likely hitting up one of the farmer's markets. Tweaking recipes, maybe."

"Dreaming up new menus for the rich and famous?"

Did she think he was just some shallow famewhore? He sidestepped her petulant question, his pride smarting a bit. She was determined to believe the worst of him. Now why was that? And why did it sting? "It's not all glitz and glamor. There's a lot of behind-the-scenes work. I also oversee the Queen's food ministry. We provide meals and nutrition counseling to families with life-challenging illnesses."

Maxine blinked; her facial expression remained unchanged. His signature program usually impressed people. But *this* woman? Crickets.

Tough crowd.

After dabbing more sweat from her face, she met his gaze. "I'm assuming you don't cook every minute. What does an executive chef do all day?"

The note of curiosity he detected in her voice sounded genuine. "The exec chef oversees the kitchen staff and operations. Planning, scheduling, training, onboarding. I'm not a huge fan of the personnel management piece, but I see the value in encouraging and inspiring the next up-and-coming generation of chefs. The Queen's Kitchen is quite prestigious on the resume. I also supervise the apprentice and internship programs."

At this, Maxine brightened and sat forward in her chair. "I didn't even know you had apprentices and interns."

Nathan could talk about this topic for hours. "The skills you learn in the kitchen can serve you for a lifetime. You'll always be employable and able to feed yourself. And you'll know how to impress a date. None of that should be an afterthought. Those are basic life skills."

"Especially the date part?"

He couldn't help but smile at that. She was just going to insist on busting his balls. "They need someone leading them who's done it, not some pencil-pushing do-gooder who's never been in the trenches."

"You're passionate about this. I bet there's quite a backstory."

"Not really," he murmured. "I imagine you did something similar so you can pretty the Queen up for a living." He'd been going for lighthearted, but Maxine's demeanor went from curious to frosty in a blink. She stiffened, her gaze hardening.

"Please don't do that." Her voice was quiet, controlled, and just this side of snippy. Her back had gone ramrod straight.

"Do what?"

"Treat my profession with derision. Saying I just pretty someone up is insulting to my artistry. I went to school just like you did to learn my craft."

Given how hostility was rolling off her, Nathan deduced that there was some heavy history here. He'd stepped in it big time. *Shit.*

"It's not just the superficial, making someone look pretty. Style is much deeper than what someone is wearing. It's a form of communication that makes statements about who you are and what you value, the image you want to project. Style is building a brand and establishing a mood or credibility. Then there's the mental and emotional health aspect that goes along with it. Styling the Queen is an honor."

Her rant spilled out in a rush, with indignation lacing every word. She was breathing hard by the time she finished, her eyes blazing. Nathan held up his hands in a conciliatory gesture. "I never thought about it that way. I apologize. I did not intend to demean you or be condescending."

Her rigid posture relaxed, but only a fraction. "This is an argument I've had more than once."

"I can tell." Nathan pulled in a deep breath. "How about we put aside this nonsense?"

Maxine shot to her feet, hands perching on her hips. "I don't think taking pride in my profession is nonsense."

"That's not what I—damn, I just can't ever seem to find my footing with you." Nathan rubbed his forehead and sighed. Where was a white flag to wave when you needed one? He just kept digging himself deeper into the hole. "I meant the nonsense of having a misunderstanding. Let's put that behind us and try something else. How would you style me?"

Another tense silence, though less so. Nathan worried she might not play along, but then she looked him over and tapped a fingertip on her lips as the wheels turned. "Of course, it depends on the image you want to project, the occasion. Some other factors. But honestly? You've got that sexy silver fox thing going for you. I'd lean into that for sure. You're all smooth polish and pretty words, but there's a subtle badass vibe in the mix, too. You have just a bit of a hard edge that's difficult to spot, like you're just skirting the limits of danger. Like by the time someone finds out about the hard edge, it's too late. You've already taken them apart. I'd play up that angle."

His eyebrows had shot up at the *sexy silver fox* description. Maxine thought he was hot? "Dangerous. I like it."

Maxine rolled her eyes, and Nathan was relieved to see her lips curve into a small smile. "You would."

"Let's say I was going to a silent auction for a favorite charity. No, a *bachelor* auction."

"With you being one of the eligible bachelors?"

Nathan nodded.

Warming to the possibilities now, Maxine rubbed her hands together and peered at him more closely. They were both still sweating, but traces of that sexy perfume she was wearing lingered. Dammit.

"Hmm. Unfortunately, most men overdo it at functions like that and end up looking like strutting peacocks. All sparkle, but no real shine. You've got something special that doesn't need ostentatious displays to stand out. I'd play everything cool and classic with a crisp black and white tuxedo. That striking contrast would be devastating on you. Peak lapels, obviously. Single button front. Maybe a houndstooth in your pocket square? Mother-of-pearl studs and cuff links set in platinum. Wing tip oxfords. Ooh, or a velvet loafer. You could pull that off easily. Broody and debonair. Oh, yeah, you'd look like a sexy spy who'd just as soon strangle you as seduce you."

That was close to how he was feeling about her right now. She was luminous as she rattled off details of her vision. "That sounds pretty badass."

"Women would lose their minds bidding on you."

Would *she*? Nathan almost asked her what kind of underwear he should wear with it just to hear her talk more about dressing him. It shouldn't have been a turn-on, but it was. He might have to pay more attention to fashion.

"So, what was with that beefcake magazine cover?"

The unexpected pivot in topic made Nathan frown. "I don't follow."

"I've seen the spreads on you in the society pages, but that was quite the departure."

Had she been keeping tabs on him the way he'd done with her? He liked the thought of that. "I was publicizing my sister's foundation launch. She wanted to raise awareness of colorectal cancer. Apparently, married men live longer because they have wives who will hector them into getting their screenings. So the real campaign was raising *women's* awareness."

"Way to capitalize on your... assets."

Ah, perhaps she liked what she'd seen. What man wouldn't puff up a little at that? "I talked her out of the bachelor auction. I've done that in the past, and it was a feeding frenzy." He gave a mock shiver. "Even if it was for a good cause."

Maxine laughed, then returned to her seat. "Okay, let's get into these games before we find something else to bicker about. Ooh, look, the conversation cards are rated by spiciness. Do we start fiery or work up to it?"

Chapter Nine

Maxine

"Dealer's choice," Nathan said, and the smile he aimed at her was like a kick. "Or we could start with truth or dare. I'm game for either."

Even though it had been her idea, Maxine hesitated, then gave what she hoped was a nonchalant shrug. "I feel like I'm back in middle school. No one ever chose me to do those kissing games."

He lifted a thick eyebrow at her. "No?"

"I was a nerdy bookworm, always drawing."

"Hey, have a little nerd pride, will you?"

"Don't tell me *you* were a nerd?"

"I was captain of the academic pentathlon team."

"The what? I've never heard of that."

Laughter danced in his eyes. "We competed with other schools on schoolwork. For fun."

Maxine burst out laughing and threw up her hands. "Okay, you got me beat. I thought for sure you were the popular jock."

"Nope. Not at all. What gave you that impression?"

"You mean you weren't always—" she motioned at his body, but he just cocked his head and affected an innocent expression.

"Always what, love?"

She bet he called every woman *love*, but that didn't stop her stomach from somersaulting. "You didn't get those muscles making basil chiffonade, that's for sure."

The pompous ass gave her a wide grin that bordered on the arrogant. Why did it seem like he was enjoying this? "You like my muscles, then?"

"Any straight woman with a pulse would like your muscles," she muttered under her breath, prompting a laugh from him. If those jeans had been a couple of inches lower....

"Come on, let's play. What've you got?"

They took turns asking each other silly, non-kissing questions until the sun went down and made it impossible to read the cards. Nathan pulled the curtains open wide to let in the light of the full moon.

Then Maxine remembered that she'd downloaded the latest murder mystery novel she'd been listening to. Since there was no hope of their cell phone batteries lasting a full two days, they might as well enjoy an audiobook while they could. Maxine was only a few chapters in, and it didn't take long to catch him up to speed. When Nathan said he preferred true crime podcasts, they debated the merits of each. Her battery died right as the mystery was getting juicy.

"Antonio did it," Nathan declared with confidence she didn't share.

Talking through the list of suspects together was entertaining. Nathan's unique way of looking at things made her suspect again that he was more than he seemed.

They lapsed into companionable silence until Maxine yawned. The heat and the dim room were making her drowsy. "Okay, I'm quite tired and ready to go to sleep."

Maxine looked over at the nest of sofa cushions and pillows with a dispassionate gaze. "Well, here goes nothing."

She had sweat through the entirety of her dress and felt bereft without the usual sights and sounds she needed to slip off to dreamland. No matter how she arranged the pillows or her body, though, she slept only in fitful stretches. She couldn't stay asleep, despite the fatigue.

Maxine scrunched herself into a ball and let out a heavy, exasperated sigh.

44

Chapter Ten

Nathan

NATHAN, TOO, FELT SLUMBER tugging at him with insistence, and he dropped off almost the moment he laid down. But Maxine repositioning herself kept jostling him awake.

His internal clock told him it was around two in the morning when he reached his limit. "Stop squirming, woman."

From her position next to him, Maxine let out an exasperated groan. "I can't get comfortable. It's too hot. I usually have a fan blowing right in my face, my sound machine on, and aromatherapy linen spray." She expelled a breath—sounding beyond frustrated. "I'm sorry, I know this is hard for you, too."

Her voice held a note of desperation, and Nathan's heart went out to her. "Nothing to apologize for. What would make you more comfortable?"

"Being naked," came the muffled response. "I don't wear clothes to bed. They make me feel like I'm being strangled. But I can't do that."

Nathan let out a chuckle. "It's dark, Maxine, and these are extraordinary circumstances. Would it make you feel better if I get naked, too?"

When she said nothing, he ventured, "Maxine?"

Her voice was small in the dark, with just a hint of a quaver. "Is this a trick question? If you're trying to get me to admit to wanting—"

"No, nothing like that. You flopping like a fish out of water is keeping me up."

"Oh. Sorry. I can't help it."

A moment of uncomfortable silence passed. "What were you worried about admitting?"

"Never mind, Chef," she muttered.

"If there's a possibility of us getting naked, even just to sleep, I think you'd better call me Nathan. I am a sexy silver fox, after all."

She groaned, but there was playfulness in it. "I'm going to regret telling you that, aren't I?

"Probably."

Her uncertainty amused him. Perhaps Ms. Abernathy wasn't quite as unaffected by his nearness as she projected. The thought made him smile in the darkness. "I've got an idea."

In the bathroom, he soaked one of the hand towels to make a cool compress. Unfortunately, the water didn't get any colder than tepid, but it was better than nothing. She let out a grateful sigh and whispered a thank you when he draped it over the back of her neck.

They ended up talking for several more hours about any and everything. Nathan tried to keep his voice monotonous. Somewhere around dawn, she fell into a solid sleep at last, doubtless from sheer exhaustion. He breathed a sigh of relief for her, for she'd seemed miserable, and he knew how cranky he got whenever circumstances disturbed his rest. He needed eight straight hours to feel human. Seeing her unhappy was twisting something up inside him.

He was an early riser—his time in the Guard made sure of that. This time though, instead of jumping up to attack the day, he let himself doze next to Maxine. She lay curled into a ball on her side, facing him, one hand tucked beneath her cheek. Her face in sleep was almost delicate. Was she ever this relaxed in her waking hours? Something told him that was unlikely. Maxine was like a force of nature.

They were out of food, and it would likely be another hot day. The rum was gone, too. She'd already told him she got hangry. He couldn't do anything about the food, but Nathan committed himself to making the best of the situation.

Chapter Eleven

Maxine

Bleary-eyed, hungry, and stiff, Maxine was out of sorts when she woke up. The pillows they'd stacked were askew. She sat up and tried to stretch the kinks from her neck and back. Nathan must be in the bathroom.

Thank goodness there were toothpaste kits in the supplies they'd found in the butler's pantry. True, the contents had yellowed with age, but vintage was better than none. Her hair must be a disaster after all that tossing and turning without a headscarf. She'd assess the damage in a moment. Thankfully, she'd hung her purse on the end of the garment rack when she came in, so she had at least a few beauty supplies.

Rummaging around in the bucket bag, Maxine looked for the compressed towel pellets she always kept on her. You just never knew when you'd have an emergency that required a washcloth. That had been a hard lesson learned after a show in Toronto. She'd been dead on her feet and had fallen asleep wearing a full face of dramatic stage makeup. She had woken up with the worst case of conjunctivitis the urgent care doctor had ever seen.

Bright Lytuan sunshine was streaming in through the floor-to-ceiling windows, and the room was already uncomfortably warm. It had cooled off a little overnight, as Nathan had predicted, but the reprieve would be short-lived. They were in for another day of steamy misery. *Fantastic.*

She must look a fright and smell dreadful. Day-old deodorant could only do so much. Thinking she'd just be in and out with the clothing drop-off, Maxine had put little effort into her attire. Now she wished she'd done the whole beauty routine, although that probably wouldn't have made a difference at the end of two days. No matter how polished she might have been when she arrived, she would still be closed up in a stuffy room with no climate control the whole weekend.

Maxine made a face. They'd gotten through one night. Hopefully, that was the worst of it. She couldn't recall what the weather forecast for the weekend had been. Sunny and hot, she suspected. Perfect beach weather was a near constant on the island when hurricane season wasn't upon them.

Nathan gave her a friendly smile when he emerged from the Queen's bathroom, and her jaw almost dropped. The man was sleep-tousled and sporting salt-and-pepper stubble. He looked so ridiculously sexy, Maxine worried her panties were going to melt off. How the hell was he not a hot rumpled mess like a normal person? There was no justice in the world. He must have read something in her expression, for his eyebrows drew together in a frown when he offered a good morning greeting.

Maxine returned it with a half-hearted grumble, excused herself, then charged into the bathroom and slammed the door behind her. She avoided looking at herself in the mirror until she'd relieved herself and brushed her teeth. Nothing could have prepared her for what she saw. She let out an involuntary shriek that brought Nathan knocking and asking if everything was okay.

Maxine threw the door open and pointed at the chaos on her head. "It looks like some sort of woodland creature is going to spring out of this rat's nest!"

Another frown pinched Nathan's brow, even as he suppressed a smile. At least he had the good sense to do that. "It's not too bad."

"Thanks, but I can hear the lie. This might take a while." Maxine dug in her purse for her hair tools and got to work, cursing in a steady stream under her breath. The comb was from when her hair was shorter, and she snarled it in the tangles in no time. She gave a cry of frustration and pain, fretting that she might have to cut it and the knots out.

Nathan cleared his throat from the doorway, bringing her attention back to her companion in this disaster. He held out a hand to her. "Will you let me try?"

She shrugged and shoved a second comb at him. "Why not? You can't make it any worse. I think I'm going to have to cut it out."

"Huh. I might surprise you."

"Anything is possible. Just be careful, will you?"

"I'm not going to hurt you, Maxine."

"You already have."

He cocked an eyebrow at her, his smile faltering. "How's that?"

"Never mind."

Before saying anything else, he circled her to assess what he was working with. She couldn't read his expression. "Okay, let's give this a shot." He motioned to the seating area. He tossed the cushions back onto the sofa and had her sit on the floor between his legs, just as she would have done with her mother or cousins or aunties.

He surprised her with the gentleness of his touch. More than that, it was competent. The man was a walking contradiction. She kept drifting off into a doze as he unwound the comb and untangled the knots with care.

"You're good at this," Maxine murmured, letting herself lean against his thighs a little. She admonished herself for noticing the corded muscle.

Nathan's chuckle was full of good humor. "Don't sound so shocked. I did my daughter's hair every morning for years."

Interesting. "Not her mom?"

A heavy silence hung in the air, and Maxine detected the slightest hesitation in his movements. "No. I had custody." He continued his methodical parting and combing of her hair. "What's the first thing you want to do when we get out of here?"

Maxine noted the smooth subject change but didn't comment on it. "Hmm. I'm going to turn the AC down as far as it will go, eat the first thing I can get my hands on, take a shower, then stand in front of the open freezer. You?"

"I just want something decent to eat that I don't have to cook. Think I'll be going straight to the Rainbow Diner."

"Ooh, I love the Rainbow! They have the best conch fritters."

Nathan groaned in longing. "What I wouldn't give for a basket of those right now."

Their stomachs rumbled almost in unison. They both laughed.

"My daughter wore one of your dresses to her wedding. She was thrilled that I know you, even just tangentially."

"You don't look old enough to have a married daughter."

"I started young and so did she. She just learned she's expecting her first."

"Your first grandbaby?"

"Yes, Ericka's my only child. I already know I'll be spoiling that kiddo rotten even before they get here."

The way his voice brightened made Maxine's heart squeeze. "That's exciting. Congratulations."

"Thanks. Would you like me to braid this for you?"

A lazy smile made its way to Maxine's lips. "You braid, too? You'd better watch out, Chef. A woman could fall for this kind of thing." Honestly, his hands felt glorious in her hair.

He put his lips close to her ear and whispered, "Would that be so bad? And you're supposed to be calling me Nathan."

A shiver went through her at the unspoken promise in his voice. It almost sounded like he was talking about something else. Things had shifted last night in more ways than one. Or was she imagining things? *Oh, dear.* Was her resolve weakening? Maxine did her best to harden her heart a little, but it was no use. It was official. She liked the man.

Shit.

Chapter Twelve

Nathan

THE TEMPERATURE IN THE room had risen to sweltering by the time Nathan finished with her hair. No cutting was required. He threw two matching cornrows in—his practiced fingers flying as he completed the style, even though it had been years since he'd last done it. It should hold for the night, leaving one less thing for her to worry about. Maxine seemed delighted with his hairdressing skills when she saw the braids in the bathroom mirror. The smile she beamed at him was so dazzling one would have thought he'd hung the moon. Her joy over such a tiny thing was intoxicating—a wonder to behold. Nathan had a difficult time tearing his gaze away from her.

A few outdated magazines and catalogs kept their attention for a while, but they both grew rather bored. Nathan made up a game where they tried to pitch pens and pencils into a crystal vase unearthed from the dark recesses of the butler's pantry. On the upside, they'd scored big, finding a solar-powered flashlight that had escaped their notice during the previous day's search. They continued with the non-spicy conversation cards, answering questions such as what they would do with fifty million dollars, what accomplishment they were most proud of, and what article of clothing they could never part with. Things escalated into potentially steamy territory when Maxine jumped ahead to investigate just how racy things would get. A series of outrageous "would you rather" scenarios had them both laughing. The spicy questions were silly, devoid of any actual heat.

Shame. Nathan would have relished the opportunity to learn more about Maxine's desires. Nathan mopped the perspiration from his brow and the back of his neck while scrutinizing Maxine's profile as she flipped through an old news magazine with listless fingers. Hot and hangry as she was, she didn't complain, which he respected. Whiny people grated on his nerves. She seemed just as eager to distract herself as he was. When they got out of here tomorrow, he was pitching the clothes he was wearing right into the rubbish bin. His T-shirt was so soaked, he could probably wring it out.

"I have a question that's not on one of those cards."

"Oh?" A twinkle of interest lit in her eyes. Nathan hesitated, disliking that he was about to extinguish it.

"What were you referring to earlier when you said I'd already hurt you?"

As he'd figured she might, Maxine closed down straightaway. A hard suspiciousness seeped into her gaze. This had been nagging at him since she'd said it, and he had a gut feeling the answer would be enlightening. When she didn't answer, he worried she'd pretend she hadn't heard.

Maxine heaved a heavy sigh and took a long time to respond. "You almost cost me this job."

Nathan stilled. "I did?"

She set the magazine aside and swiveled to face him. "They only hired me on a provisional basis, and you ruined my best shot. That dress was my audition piece, and my assistants and I put everything else aside to focus on it." She crossed her legs and smoothed her hands along her thighs, straightening her skirt hem. "I'd just started my own design house. That was my first big break. It couldn't get any bigger, right?"

Well, shit. It would have stung less if she'd punched him in the gut. She was trying to sound nonchalant about it, but he picked up on the undercurrent of hurt in her voice. She fidgeted with the edge of a page, curling and uncurling it. "I didn't realize that." Sure, his incredible cake had been wrecked, but he hadn't been in any danger of losing his job over it. Or of not *getting* his job because of it. And here he'd been acting like *he* was the aggrieved party for two years. Damn, no wonder she always looked like she wanted to flay him. Who would blame her? "That must have been a veritable nightmare."

She arched an eyebrow at him. If looks could kill, he'd be six feet under and pushing up daisies for sure. "Seeing the best work I'd ever done covered in chocolate fondant and rendered unwearable? Yes. Yes, it was a nightmare."

Nathan couldn't help the grimace. "It was ganache, but I take your point." *Stop talking, Nathan.* The woman had just bared her soul, and he was correcting her culinary terminology? He was an ass. "I'm sorry. Truly. I had no idea." He sat forward in his chair until she met his gaze. "For what it's worth from a lowly chef, the Queen always looks amazing. And I don't know crap about fashion."

She softened, her facial features relaxing a smidgen. He even got a sliver of a smile. "Thank you. I appreciate that." She chewed on her lower lip. "You're anything but a lowly chef. I've tasted your creations. They are otherworldly."

Nathan was an excellent chef—one who'd won top honors and Michelin stars. Not one of those accolades was as meaningful as Maxine's compliment. Something intangible bloomed and cracked open between them, giving him hope. Hope for what, though, he didn't know.

Chapter Thirteen

MAXINE SNAPPED AWAKE AND lay in the disorienting near darkness, wondering what had disturbed her. It had taken forever to fall asleep, but she got the feeling she hadn't been asleep long. Nathan was no longer beside her. The vibration in the air felt... wrong, like something was amiss. She looked around the office but couldn't discern much in the low light.

There.

An out-of-place sound. Not the water running in the bathroom. A gut feeling made her hesitate before calling out. She padded barefoot to the bathroom and peered inside the cracked door. In front of the vanity mirror, Nathan stood with his eyes closed, his broad back faintly visible in the moonlight. Something was very wrong, though. His whole body was rigid and shaking, all traces of good humor absent. He leaned on tightly clenched fists, gulping for air like he couldn't get enough. His head hung, and sweat poured from his face.

Maxine moved into the room without hesitation, laying a comforting hand between his shoulder blades, the other on his wrist. His skin was hot to the touch. She flicked the faucet handle to turn the water off.

She had to call his name twice before he opened his eyes. Nothing could have prepared her for the voracity of his gaze. It seared into her with a heartbreaking mixture of pleading and shame, embarrassment and rage. The intensity was overwhelming, enough to make her want to back up a step, but Maxine held on instead, for she recognized this. She was intimately acquainted with this type of pain. She alternated tapping his back and forearm, counting softly in a low, even tone as she did so. When she reached twenty-four, she stopped to pull in a series of long, deep breaths that filled up her belly, urging Nathan to do the same.

He started to come back in the second set, his ragged breathing evening out. She nodded as he matched her breathing pattern. The tension in his body unwound before her eyes, his posture softening. By the time he was counting and breathing along with her, they were face-to-face, his hands in hers.

Maxine didn't look away, even with the panic brimming in his beautiful eyes. She did her best to exude calm and acceptance. When he was back to himself, she wet a paper towel, rung it out, then wiped the sweat from his brow. His eyes drifted closed while he drew in a shuddering breath, longer and deeper than the rest, but they were clear when he opened them again. He didn't shut it all off at once. It was far too late for that, and she realized what a monumental effort it must have taken for him to trust her with his exposed pain.

Nathan rolled his shoulders, rocked back and forth on the balls of his feet, then spread and closed his fingers a few times. Grounding himself, she thought.

He caught her hand before she could turn away and curved it around his stubbled cheek. He nuzzled into it the tiniest bit, then murmured a thank you. Maxine's stomach did a slow roll. His eyes searched hers, and he must have seen the understanding there.

"So." His voice was low and hoarse. She wouldn't have heard it if they weren't standing so close. He cleared his throat and tried again. "So, you've seen this before or had them yourself."

Maxine pulled her hand back before she gave into the urge to stroke his face. "Panic attacks? Both. I was in a car accident that killed my father. A drunk driver hit us when we were off-island, and we were trapped together in the wreckage for a few hours. It was a rural road. We'd overturned in a ditch. He didn't die right away. But I couldn't get out to help. Not him or my brother—he was just a toddler at the time. My leg was broken. I screamed and cried for help until I had no voice, but no one came until the next day. My father... he was gone by then. We'd been quarreling. The last thing I'd said right before the crash was that I hated him. I was such a brat. Classic story, right?" She could say the words now without falling apart, but it had taken a long time to get there.

"How old were you?"

"Eight."

"Christ. That's horrible. I'm sorry."

Her smile was wan. "It was a rural town. The police and firefighters didn't speak Lytuan. I didn't speak any Igbo, and this was well before language apps and cell phones. My mother had been sick with worry when we didn't come back to the inn that night. She was there at the station, reporting us missing.

"I had nightmares and panic attacks for years. My brother, too. We tried a lot of different methods to cope. The therapists thought it was because I'd felt so out of control when the accident happened. I was helpless and to this day, I hate feeling that way."

His nostrils flared, and his eyes widened, conveying the root of at least some of his pain. "She didn't blame you, did she? Your mother?"

Maxine shook her head. "Oh, no, nothing like that." She decided she wouldn't pick at the wound right now and didn't ask what caused his current attack. "Whether it happened yesterday or ten years ago, trauma has a way of rearing its head, piling on when we're in a weakened condition and emotions are high."

Nathan grunted and offered a half smile. "Like being trapped someplace with no escape?"

"And feeling helpless? Winner, winner, chicken dinner."

Once they'd returned to their nest of pillows, Nathan asked, "Are you and your brother close?"

That pain was closer to the surface. Maxine had to steel herself against the onslaught of emotion that hit with thoughts of Shawn. Her stomach tightened with it. "I wish. He... chose a different path."

Nathan cocked his head and regarded her, discerning something in her voice she hadn't meant to disclose. "Drugs or alcohol?"

"Both."

"I'm sorry. That's tough. My ex ended up needing inpatient treatment for alcohol a couple of times. Addiction is a terrible thing. Not only for the person with the addiction, but for everyone who cares about them."

A tender moment of shared understanding of that particular grief spun out, connecting them. "I've always tried to keep my wing over my niece," Maxine said. "She's at university."

Maxine sniffed and dashed a tear away before it could roll down her cheek. She stretched out and settled down again, though Nathan remained sitting, his elbow propped on a bent knee.

Her suspicion that there was more proved correct some minutes later. In the quiet stillness of the night, Nathan ventured, "You asked how I knew so much about the Queen's office."

Maxine was silent for a long moment, her attention sharpening. "Yes."

"I was an Elite Guard with the previous Queen. Until I failed in my duties and got my partner killed. *Then* I became a chef."

Chapter Fourteen

MAXINE COULDN'T HELP THE startled gasp that escaped her. She remained still, though, with her heart pounding against her chest and wondering if she should prod him to continue or just wait. She'd counted seven heartbeats in the silence before Nathan spoke again.

"Angel was my mentor and a friend. I was partnered with her for most of the eleven years I was an Elite Guard. We were overseas with the previous Queen and her granddaughters, Sophia and Samera. They were teenagers at the time, and well, we lost them. They snuck out to go clubbing. I was furious and out of patience as we tracked them down. I'd just had another big fight on the phone with my own moody teenager who hated me. The last thing I wanted to do was chase down two more inconsiderate, ungrateful kids. All typical teen behavior, but I was pretty much done with anyone under the age of eighteen. In the morning, I was hungover and still pissed. Angel took one look at me and ordered me back to my hotel room. My head wasn't in the right place, and she knew it. She covered for me with the rest of the team.

"So, she was there with the Queen during the assassination attempt on the prime minister she was visiting. Angel was standing in my place, and she died for it."

Despite the oppressive heat, goosebumps broke out up and down Maxine's arms. She dragged in a ragged breath, tears stinging the backs of her eyes.

"She didn't tell anyone the real reason I wasn't there. Just said I wasn't feeling well. They shot her like a dog."

The anguish in his voice tore at her heart. "Oh, Nathan," Maxine whispered.

Nathan got up and went to stand at the window. "It was quick. She didn't suffer." He glanced down at his clenched fists and stuffed them in his pockets.

His casual stance did not fool Maxine. His entire demeanor was heavy with grief and self-recrimination.

He huffed out a breath and shook his head. "Anyway, I retired from the Guard after that. I'd lost my edge. I wasn't on duty where I was supposed to be, and Angel paid the price. She and her husband... they'd been talking about adopting a child. I still have difficulty looking him in the eye. If I'd been there—"

"You would have died instead? Who's to say if that's actually what would have happened? Maybe you both would have been killed. Or neither of you."

"Maxine—"

"No." She hurried over to him, and it took everything in her not to take his face in her hands and kiss his hurt away. "You can't know that. No one can know that." She stopped short of offering feel-good platitudes. These were demons only Nathan himself could lay to rest.

Nathan blew out a breath. "Okay, it's clear we need to lighten things up. Let's get back into one of these games."

Maxine hesitated, peering at his face in the bright moonlight. "You're okay?"

The heartbreaking shadows in his eyes gutted her, but there was hope there, too. He nodded and drew her closer with a hand on her elbow. He was on the verge of saying something. Whatever it was, he decided against it and feathered his fingers over her cheek instead. Something potent passed between them then, spurred by the burgeoning intimacy from their earlier interaction. Maxine's skin tingled beneath his touch.

Before she could speak or give in to the sudden urge to lay one on him, Nathan stepped away and dropped his hand. He went back to the sofa cushions and picked up the cards.

Message received. He was done talking about it. Maxine had to say something now, or it would be awkward later. "Thank you for sharing that with me. Did you get solid mental health support?"

"Oh, yes. The Guard takes care of its people."

The lingering sadness in his posture dissipated after several rounds of silly questions. Maxine continued to chew their interactions over. No wonder he was so quick to take charge when things had gone wrong. Those observations she'd had about how he assessed things made perfect sense now.

They decided on one more round before settling down to go back to sleep. Maxine's breath hitched when she read the next card to herself. Then she hurriedly shuffled it to the back of the pile to draw another.

Nathan spotted the move and called her out on her shenanigans. "Hold up. What was that?"

"We're not doing that one."

"That's not how the game works."

"Trust me on this. That one's nothing but trouble."

"Well, now I *have* to see it. Hand it over." Nathan held his palm up and made a gimme motion.

Maxine retrieved the card and passed it to him with reluctance. Her hand trembled.

Nathan chuckled as he read the short missive, then set it aside. "You're the one who thought they were missing out on this game before. I dare you to come kiss me."

She hesitated, weighing her options. *Oh, just get it over with already,* Maxine chided herself. She leaned in, pecked him on the lips, and pulled away with a nervous laugh.

"Is that the best you can do? Come on, Maxine, where's your nerve? Unless you're ready to forfeit."

"And give you the satisfaction? Never." Her competitive streak spoke before her common sense could. It must be the hunger. This was heading for trouble.

"Then quit stalling and kiss me like you mean it. Take a risk."

He had a point. She *had* bemoaned not being able to play this game properly. But he didn't think she would do it, did he? She'd show him. With new determination, Maxine pushed him against the base of the sofa and climbed onto his lap to straddle his thighs. Even in the dim light, she saw the heat flare in his eyes. She took his chin and brushed her lips against his once, twice, then took the plunge. The warning bells going off in her mind like the klaxons of yesterday didn't stop her.

His hands tightened on her waist, then slid up her back. Her heart was pounding, and heat was pooling in her core when she sat back. Dazed and breathing hard, Maxine wondered what the hell had gotten into her. She'd just kissed the hot chef!

"Well, that was acceptable," he said.

"*Acceptable*?" Her protest came out as a squawk. Affronted, she shoved at his shoulder. "You—"

Her indignant tirade died away when Nathan cupped the back of her neck and drew her to him again. His smile told her he was kidding. He stroked his thumb under her jaw, leaving the skin tingling. Maxine shivered. "Your mouth is so soft and pretty. Like the ripest berries waiting to be plucked and savored. I've had one hell of a time trying not to stare at it."

Maxine's eyes widened, and her breath caught in her throat. A thrill shot right down to her empty belly. *Oh, shit.*

He rolled her under him into the collection of cushions, throwing her off balance in more ways than one. His massive body covering and pressing down on hers notched her sudden arousal up even higher. The fabric of his jeans was rough against her inner thighs where the skirt of her dress had rucked up. He searched her face, prolonging the start of another brain-searing kiss.

Seeing only invitation and not a bit of trepidation, Nathan took control, his hands cradling her face as their lips met once more. His kiss was the stuff of fantasies—long and deep, slow and sexy. Somewhere beyond the polite uncertainty that came with a first kiss and the easy familiarity of established lovers. Nathan kissed her with authority—like they'd been doing so for years. His tongue slid over hers in the most tantalizing way—teasing and sensual and just enough.

They were clinging to each other when they drew apart. His eyes were dark and full of mystery as they met hers, desire swirling in their depths. Maxine licked her lips and watched his gaze lower to her mouth.

"Where did *that* come from?" Her voice sounded like it didn't belong to her at all—husky and breathy. Her heart was thundering against her ribcage.

He gave her upper lip a gentle nip, and Maxine almost moaned. "If I was honest with either one of us, I would have asked you out on a date a long time ago. But I'm too old for you."

"Just how old do you think I am?"

Nathan nuzzled the tender skin beneath her chin and let out a low chuckle. "I'm not falling into that trap."

"I'm thirty-eight and I think you should kiss me again. We should make sure that wasn't a fluke."

"As you wish. And gladly."

It wasn't a fluke.

Time melted away. Maxine was so hot and bothered she was ready to start tearing their clothes off. All her brain cells seemed to short out. No one had ever made her crave more the way Nathan did. Shaken to her core, Maxine excused herself to retreat to the bathroom, where she could pull herself together. Goodness, if those consuming kisses had taken place anywhere but here? All bets would have been off.

The man wore a smirk—clearly satisfied with himself—when she returned. It made her laugh. He had top-notch skills in the kissing department, that was for sure. She had difficulty remembering what day it was.

Their banter grew more flirtatious when they picked the game up again. Nathan was funny. Laughing kept her mind off the gnawing hunger.

"Ooh, here's a good one," Maxine said. "What's something you want right now that you know you can't have?"

"Ah, Maxine, love, that's easy. I want to bury myself inside that lush body of yours and make you scream my name all night."

Maxine was rarely rendered speechless; Nathan's frank talk surprised her into silence. Oh, he was a bold one. She just knew he'd make good on that promise. Heat and want curled through her like ink in water. She fanned her face, feeling the flush of desire there. With the taste of him still on her tongue, she was a heartbeat away from going to her knees before him and tugging those jeans down. *Get ahold of yourself!* She was glad for the cover of darkness, so he couldn't see just how hot his words made her.

Maxine considered as she tried to get comfortable and go back to sleep. Was their intense physical reaction due to the circumstances, or was there more substance to it?

The heat and her libidinous thoughts wouldn't allow her to rest. She tossed and turned for the better part of an hour before abandoning the effort. "Does the offer to get naked still stand? I'm all done with suffering for propriety's sake."

"You're safe with me. Get comfortable and get some rest." Nathan turned the flashlight off, plunging the room into further darkness.

Maxine was very aware of Nathan's breathing as she stripped off her dress and undergarments. She was much more comfortable when she lay down again, but she couldn't get his words out of her mind. They would definitely circle back to that conversation when they weren't trapped.

Chapter Fifteen

Nathan

NATHAN AWOKE WARM AND content just after daybreak. He thought pleasant dreams were the cause until he felt something tickling the underside of his chin, and he pried open his eyelids. He and Maxine were curled together, their legs intertwined, and her face tucked into the crook of his neck. His hand was resting on her lower back.

Her *naked* back.

What the—

He snatched his hand away, but she nuzzled against him, burrowing into his warmth with a soft sigh. Nathan closed his eyes again for just a moment and let himself savor the luscious feel of her generous curves against him. The temptation to kiss her awake was strong. The desire to lay her out like a feast before him and devour her was even stronger. God, he wanted to touch her, to skim his fingertips over all that smooth skin, but he wasn't an asshole who took advantage. Nathan disentangled himself and got up.

A beautiful woman lying naked in his arms, and he was backing away. What was the world coming to?

Now if the attraction was still there when they *weren't* trapped and being steamed like oysters, then that was a different matter altogether. It had been almost impossible to keep his hands to himself while they were kissing. She'd been like a live wire beneath him, and he'd wanted all she had to give.

Nathan's hands shook as he pulled down one of the curtains to cover Maxine's nudity. She stirred a little when he draped the gauzy material over her, but she didn't wake. He could still see the shape of her, every mouthwatering curve. This woman.

Any moment now, she'd wake up and start sassing him. He couldn't wait.

He sat across from where she lay and studied her face, noting the weariness in it, even as she slept on. They'd be getting out of here sometime today. With any luck, she'd be good as new once she was back in her own home. His solid sleep was a surprise. Most times, he either slept like shit or not at all after an episode.

A muted, nervous energy still churned throughout his body. Something fundamental had shifted between the two of them last night. Being vulnerable under the cover of darkness was easy, but would that intimate connection remain after they reverted to their regular routines?

The panic attack had come on with blinding speed, or perhaps he'd missed the usual warning signs. When had his last one been? So long ago that he couldn't recall the coping techniques he'd learned when they'd been a more frequent occurrence. Whatever Maxine had done with the tapping and breathing cycles was worth learning more about.

She'd come to his aid, revealed her own deep pain, and listened as he spilled out his shameful secret. No one knew the complete story about Angel except his therapist, and it had taken quite some time to build up to that confession.

Whenever anyone got anywhere close to the subject, Nathan would deflect and steer the conversation in another, safer direction. A nagging feeling in the pit of his stomach told him that wouldn't work with Maxine.

Thoughts of distracting her brought back the memory of her mouth on his. Those had been some scorching kisses. Kisses that promised soaked sheets and pleasure-filled nights. Nathan's cock stirred again, and he had to adjust how he was sitting.

He'd misjudged Maxine and was now forced to reconsider the new information that she had brought to light. He'd been an asshole. He cringed, thinking back to how cavalierly he'd behaved at the time of their run-in. Accidents happened—they could overlook that part. But he'd minimized and dismissed her. That was bullshit, and he needed to consider how he would make that up to her.

When she woke up, perhaps he'd suggest they try to start over. Nathan chided himself. His reasons weren't altruistic. He slanted a glance at her profile again. He'd been fighting an attraction to this woman ever since they met. Now that *maybe* the gigantic obstacle was out of the way, they could see if there was anything between them.

Huh. This was quite a turn from what he'd expected from this fiasco.

He amended his previous assessment of Maxine being too much work for anything beyond casual. Nathan was too seasoned to play games; he knew what he wanted and the traits he admired in women. He was liking Maxine more and more.

Rustling drew his attention. Maxine had awakened and was wrapping herself up in the curtain. She sat up in the scattered pillows and gave him a shy smile. "Thanks for this."

"No problem." Nathan unfolded himself from the sofa and turned around so she could put her clothes back on. The little sounds of fabric scraping across her skin had his imagination in overdrive.

He re-hung the curtain once she had finished dressing. Nathan didn't like the awkwardness in the air. "Why don't you go get cleaned up first?"

They set about tidying the Queen's office. It was all inconsequential small talk, as though it would break the spell if they mentioned those kisses. The calendar entry didn't list the lockdown test ending time, so they settled in to wait to get sprung.

Despite the excitement of the night before, the ordeal weighed on them. Nathan coaxed Maxine to drink some water and exert as little energy as possible. She stretched out on the reassembled sofa and threw an arm over her eyes. The minutes ticked by, as if in slow motion, with neither of them talking much. Heat-induced lethargy won the day.

When Maxine's stomach gave another pronounced growl, Nathan got an idea. "How does making a pit stop in the kitchen before going home sound?"

Maxine lifted her arm and cracked an eye open to peer at him. "I thought you didn't want to cook anything."

"No cooking," he clarified. "There'll be something we can grab from the breakfast area, even if it's just fruit or cereal bars."

"Sounds like a plan." She gave a weak laugh when his stomach gave an answering growl.

Just past two in the afternoon, the lights flickered back on, and the air conditioning unit started up. Nathan and Maxine exchanged a glance. Their rescue must be imminent. Relief flooded Nathan.

Sure enough, the electronic locks chirped a short while later. A gaggle of chattering techs spilled into the room, each falling silent as they spotted Nathan and Maxine. The lead tech demanded to know why everyone had stopped when she, too, saw that the office was not empty.

"What the heck?" She asked.

Nathan laughed a little at her confusion. "We got locked in."

"You've been in here the whole time? With no comms, no electricity?"

"Correct."

"I'm surprised you didn't murder each other."

No truer words, Nathan thought. Had everyone noticed their friction?

Nathan cut off the tech's questions after a few minutes, telling her she'd have to follow up over email. They were hungry, grubby, and itching to go home. The scruff on his face rasped when he scratched at it. He'd never appeared so disheveled in public.

To Maxine, he said, "Let's get out of here."

"Agreed."

They headed straight for the breakfast area in the kitchen, where Nathan grabbed a handful of granola bars and pointed at a basket of fruit on the counter. "This should hold us."

He peeled an orange while watching Maxine choose an apple and take several bites. Between the two of them, they polished off four of the granola bars. The moment felt oddly intimate—standing there huddled over their snacks together. They gave twin sighs of satisfaction when they were done but were both too wiped out to laugh.

"Where did you park?" Nathan wadded up her trash with his and tossed it all in the rubbish bin.

"Level B."

"I'll walk you down."

On the way, she gave him a friendly shoulder bump in the elevator that made him smile. He wasn't too tired to appreciate her flirtation. He followed her when they got off on the floor below where he'd parked his car.

Maxine slowed to a stop in the middle of the garage, frowning.

"What's wrong?"

She turned in a circle, her eyebrows knitted together. "My car is gone. I parked it—" She slapped a hand to her forehead. "Oh, Lord, they towed it. How could I—my cell phone battery is dead. I need to go back inside."

Nathan caught her arm when she turned to head back. "Can you deal with the car later? You look like you're about to fall over. I'll take you home. I can call in a favor and have it delivered to your home." He still had some sway with the Guard staff.

"I live an hour away."

"Don't worry, I'll get it there."

"That would be amazing. I don't want to put you to any trouble, though."

Nathan was already leading her back to the elevator. "It's no trouble."

"I want nothing more than to eat something cold, shower, and collapse in my own bed."

"I hear you on that."

Exhaustion precluded small talk on the ride. Nathan lowered all the windows as soon as they were inside the car, given how gross and musty he felt. He must have stunk to high heaven.

They made the drive in 45 minutes, and Maxine directed him to park in the driveway of her tidy townhouse. Nathan walked her to her door, though she insisted it wasn't necessary. There was a brief moment of awkwardness when he wasn't sure what to do. Then she was inside after a murmured thank you.

After the door closed, Nathan made a face. He'd wanted to kiss her again, touch her, something, make some physical connection, but the timing had felt... wrong.

The last two days had been both heaven and hell. Right now, though, Nathan was bone-weary and not in any shape to consider this unfamiliar territory they were navigating. He needed food, a shower, and a shave. Then a few laps in the rooftop infinity pool and a solid nap.

He'd think about everything else—including sexy Maxine—later. Once he'd had an opportunity to refresh.

Chapter Sixteen

Maxine

S HE HADN'T EXPECTED HIM to apologize. At least he seemed to get it, which was no small thing. Perhaps if she'd been less of a spiteful hardhead, she could have told him what had been at stake that fateful day. Then they could have moved past the incident long before now. What might that have looked like?

Nathan might be cocky, but he'd never struck her as unfeeling. Not really. She'd thought of him as a jerk, but deep down, suspected differently. Maybe she'd kept him at arm's distance for just that reason, that he might be too easy to like. He *was* charming, and she'd never even tried to deny that she found him attractive.

She called Dennis and got an earful of his worry and concern while she ate mint chocolate chip ice cream right out of the carton. Maxine's heart sang as she listened to the enthusiasm in his voice as he recounted the experience. His show had been a smashing success, and the Sunday event went as planned. Dennis had thought she was testing him. Nothing major in the way of accidents had transpired. He was full of sympathy for her ordeal. Maxine left out the kissing part of the story.

"I'm so proud of you, Dennis. Sorry I couldn't be there."

"Couldn't have done it without your support."

When they hung up, Maxine was restless. She needed to go shopping, do household things—all manner of administrative tasks she saved for weekends. But all she could do was savor the memory of how fantastic Nathan's lips had felt on her own. Intense, yes, but not rough like she'd imagined they would be. Come to think of it, why did she think that of him?

She hadn't wanted to seem too eager, but she wished she'd just asked for his number to text him. Instead, she had hightailed it into her house. Hmm—what was textspeak for *I want to lick up your abs?*

Dammit, she was still hot and bothered.

She'd wanted to jump him, but hesitated, knowing that what had transpired did so in part because of the unusual circumstances. What would she do now that forced proximity wasn't a factor?

Maxine unbraided her cornrows while the shower heated. She shivered, remembering Nathan's hands in her hair, the whisper of his lips by her ear as he teased her about falling for him.

After showering off the weekend grime and washing her hair, she filled the tub and added scented bath gel. Now she wanted to spoil herself and relax. This was an extra she only rarely indulged in.

Pondering the hot chef and his even hotter kisses was at the top of her list.

Maxine slid into the bathtub so that the bubbles came up to her chin. Inhaling deeply, she let the wafting lavender soothe her. They'd had a few enjoyable spells over the last two days, some even outright fun. And mercy, those kisses had been hot enough to fuse her brain cells together. They may have been goofing around, but there was nothing silly about those kisses. Until this disaster, she would have counted Nathan Olivier among her enemies. Now he was what? Besides fuel for her fantasies, that is. Would he regret telling her about his past?

A hopeful feeling welled up inside her, buoying her spirit. She hoped not.

Perhaps she could swing by the employee cafeteria. *And then what?* she admonished herself. Just blithely ask how he was feeling about things? If he'd like to pick up where they'd left off?

She was working her favorite scented moisturizer into her skin when a knock sounded at her door. Puzzled, she threw on her floral silk bathrobe and went to see who it was.

Her heart turned over in her chest when she saw Nathan standing on her doorstep through the peephole. A thrill of anticipation shot through her. She secured the knot on her robe with unsteady hands. Oh, mercy, she hadn't even started on her hair yet. He always caught her at her absolute worst.

She offered a warm hello when she opened the door. It felt like she couldn't take a full breath. He hadn't been home yet and was every bit as delicious as she remembered in the gray T-shirt and jeans. Wouldn't that sexy stubble make for the most exquisite torture against the inside of her thighs? Imagining it made her knees feel wobbly.

He proffered a brown paper bag. "I got you something."

"What's this?"

"Conch fritters from the Rainbow. This batch is uncooked, so you can just pop them in the oven or air fryer and make them fresh."

Pleasure flooded her as she accepted the bag. "That was very thoughtful. Thank you. I was going to swing by tomorrow for lunch." The air felt charged. Her heart was thundering in her chest. "Would you like to come in?"

"Yes. No. I—no." He broke eye contact, his expression pained.

She cocked her head and smiled. "Which is it?"

His face contorted into a frown as he scrubbed a hand up and down the back of his neck. "I want to, but I can't. You look good enough to eat, and I haven't had a shower yet."

She became acutely aware of having nothing on under the thin robe. There was an exhilarating hunger in his eyes as he looked her over from head to toe. When his gaze slid to her breasts, Maxine held her breath. Could he see how her nipples had hardened?

His gaze lifted to her face again. "Can I call you sometime?"

She nodded, relief spilling through her, and watched as he put her phone number into his contacts as she recited it.

After they'd said goodbye and he was about to leave, Nathan paused. He stood on her doorstep, frowned up—as though he was forging an internal debate. Conflict was in his eyes.

"Nathan?" She couldn't even get her voice above a whisper. "Was there something else?" *Please, God, let there be something else.*

She heard him mutter, "Fuck it." Then he was backing her into the hallway, and his mouth was swooping down on hers.

Thank God.

Maxine moaned into the kiss and returned it with equal fervor. Up on her tiptoes, she slid her arms around his neck. His body was hot up against her own and hard everywhere. He kicked the door shut and didn't let up as he crowded her into the wall.

Nathan drove a hand into her wet hair and closed his fist. Then he was dropping sweet kisses along her throat, the friction of his stubble pulling a hum of pleasure from deep within Maxine.

"Christ, you smell delicious. What is that—jasmine?"

"Magnolia." She was tingling everywhere and on the verge of doing something reckless.

He pulled back a little and let go of her hair, leaving her scalp tingling. "It suits you. Not gonna lie. I don't wanna stop, but this is new and, as I mentioned, I haven't had a shower."

She opened her mouth, but he shook his head. "If you tell me I can take a shower here, I won't make it two minutes before I tear this robe off you so I can taste you." As if to illustrate the point, he drew a lazy circle around one of her puckered nipples with a fingertip. The silk rasped against her sensitive flesh, making her shiver. When he did the same to the other one, her back arched, a low moan escaping her parted lips. He gave her a wicked little smile. "I want to kiss and suck these. And every inch of the rest of you."

Truthfully, Maxine was just about ready to shimmy out of the robe, tackle him to the floor, and mount him right there. But he was right. This was shiny new and needed a chance to breathe. She wouldn't be jumping into bed with the tempting Chef Nathan, no matter how dizzy and weak his kisses made her feel.

He stepped back and let his hand fall from her needy, achy nipples to his side. Maxine came close to moaning again. Her body didn't give a fig what her mind thought was best. The greedy hedonist in her wanted him to bend her over something and plow her with all that virility unleashed, pulling her hair while he did it.

Maxine suppressed a whimper. She was making a beeline for her goodie drawer the second he left.

"I'll see you when you get back."

Back? Where was she going? Heavens, now she was imagining herself on her knees for him, his hands fisted in her hair while he watched and encouraged her with dirty talk. Maxine bet Nathan had a filthy mouth that would turn her inside out. Her fingers twitched.

"From Quebec?" He grinned, as though he could read her thoughts.

"Quebec. Right." Yes, that's where she was going.

Her brain reasserted its dominance over her body, and she restrained herself when he gave her a gentle kiss goodbye.

Maxine closed the door behind him and sagged against it. She let out a long, shaky breath. Then she ran to her bedroom to relieve the gnawing ache that had built inside her.

The hot chef was going to be trouble, alright. No doubt about it.

Chapter Seventeen

Nathan

IF HE'D LET HER answer—if she'd said anything other than *fuck off*, Nathan would have tugged that flimsy robe from Maxine's body and taken her hard. Right there, up against her goddamned foyer wall.

Back inside his car, Nathan couldn't keep the huge, shit-eating grin off his face.

That damn skimpy thing hadn't disguised Maxine's lushness at all. Seeing her nipples hardened against the material had almost done him in. And those curves he couldn't stop thinking about since he'd gotten a taste of her last night. He'd wanted to ease that robe open and take his time letting his gaze roam over her. He was certain she wasn't wearing anything beneath it; that thought was why his dick was still brick hard. With her beautiful brown skin so fragrant and softer than he could have imagined, he could have lost himself in her for days.

Nathan let out a groan and had to shift in his seat. Thank goodness common sense had prevailed. It was way too soon for them to be getting intimate, no matter what his libido wanted. They couldn't stand the sight of each other just 48 hours ago. He wasn't as randy as he was in his younger days, but Nathan liked to believe his skill more than made up for it. He'd mellowed enough with age to appreciate how a single mind-blowing bout of lovemaking in a night was miles better than several instances of *pretty good*. Quality over quantity was a notion a real man understood, whereas instant gratification remained the realm of inexperienced boys.

Maxine was only a few years younger than he was, but he needed to clue her in so they could manage their expectations.

If he'd learned anything over the years, it was how to be a patient, generous, and thorough lover. He could be satisfied getting off only once and spending the rest of the night pleasuring his partner.

Hmm. All night wrapped in Maxine. Now *that* was a mouthwatering prospect. What would she sound like when she came apart in his arms?

If things kept on this upward trajectory, he might just be lucky enough to find out.

Chapter Eighteen

SHE WOULD HAVE BEEN toast if it weren't for her exacting standards in prepping for out-of-town wardrobing. If anyone noticed her preoccupation, no one said anything to Maxine.

The four days in Quebec dragged by, despite the city being one of her favorite places. Maxine had never been so eager to get back to Lytua.

Everything reminded her of Nathan. She didn't expect to *miss* the man. They exchanged a few sporadic texts when their busy schedules allowed. Maxine spent more time than she cared to admit ruminating on their time together. They'd shared a genuine connection, hadn't they? Or was it all a by-product of the circumstances?

The giddy, freefalling feeling in her stomach indicated otherwise.

Crushes and infatuation were for moony-eyed coeds. Yet the stern talking-to she gave herself didn't stop her fanciful, runaway thoughts. Nor did it dissuade the tingling when she thought of those molten kisses.

By the time the jet touched down, she'd formed a simple plan of action. Maxine would send a casual text to let him know she was back home. Then maybe she would swing by the employee cafeteria—if time permitted and nerves didn't overtake her.

She was heading toward the elevator after a debrief meeting with the Queen and Joanne when she bumped into the object of her fascination.

Nathan steadied her with hands on her shoulders.

"Hi." It came out as a breathy whisper. Maxine cleared her throat and tried again. It came out more naturally, despite her hammering heart. He looked even better than she remembered, standing there in his whites.

"Hi."

The way his eyes crinkled when he smiled at her—mercy. Prior to their time trapped together, she'd have greeted him with a reflexive scowl. Maxine could feel the sappy smile taking over her face. Oh, she had it bad.

"The Queen just left for Parliament."

He shook his head as he released her. "Actually, I was looking for you. Welcome back. Are you feeling better?"

Heat rushed to her face, then all over. "Much. All recovered. You? How was the summit?"

They were blocking the hallway, and he jostled closer when he moved to allow a couple of staff people to go around them. The hand he placed on her bare forearm seared like a brand. With her back against the wall now, Maxine tried to control her breathing and hold onto her scattering thoughts.

"You look beautiful." The way his gaze slid over her—from her Bantu knots down to the royal blue sheath dress she wore—had her pulse going haywire.

Maxine could only stammer her thanks. Had she taken extra care in getting dressed this morning on the off chance she might see him? Oh, hell yes, she had.

"I did some thinking while you were gone."

She could barely drag her gaze away from his full lips. "Oh? About what?"

"You. Me." He eased closer to her, spiking her heart rate even more. "Kisses hot enough to melt the sun."

Nathan braced a hand on the wall next to her head and leaned in. He smelled incredible. His cologne or shower gel was a subtle blend of woodsy foliage—like the forest after a rainstorm. Maxine rubbed her thighs together, cursing inwardly at being turned on in public. But he was just getting started.

He brushed the backs of his fingers over her cheek, and Maxine fought the urge to suck his thumb into her mouth. She wanted to curl her tongue around it like it was his cock.

"I tried to dismiss what happened between us as just extraordinary circumstances. But I can't get you off my mind. I want to see you again on purpose. I know you don't date where you work, but I'd like to point out that we don't actually work together."

Between his words and his voice being even deeper than she remembered, red-hot need gathered in her core. Maxine was afraid if she tried to say anything, she'd blurt out something like, "Take me to the nearest closet and fuck my brains out."

"Here's what I'm thinking." Nathan leaned in closer still so that his body was touching hers. Maxine nearly whimpered. "I'd like to cook you dinner tomorrow. My loft in the city has a marvelous view. Shit, that sounds like a line. But it's not." He gave an uneasy laugh. "I don't want to go back to us sniping and snarling at each other. I want to look at you over a candlelit table. Straight on, instead of out of the corner of my eye."

Maxine would have melted into a puddle if not for the wall holding her up. Somehow her voice still worked. "I have plans tomorrow, but how about Friday?"

"Perfect."

Emboldened, she curved her hand around the back of his neck. "I'm a pescatarian. Can you handle that?"

His eyes narrowed at the unspoken challenge in her words. "Babe, I can handle anything you throw my way." He almost kissed her. She could see his eyes darken with the intent. Then he seemed to remember they were in a place of business and had no privacy. If they were alone, she'd already have him naked and in her mouth. "I can't seem to keep my hands or lips to myself around you. I'll behave at dinner, my word."

"I... better get going."

A polite throat clearing shattered the moment, and they snapped back from one another like teenagers caught necking. A young-looking aide pushing a hand truck laden with boxes was trying to get through the hallway. He was biting his lip, his eyes downcast. Maxine almost felt sorry for him.

Nathan, though, smiled and apologized. To Maxine, he gave a two-finger salute and a wink. "I'll see you Friday, then."

And with that, he was gone, leaving her to get herself back together for the rest of the day.

Chapter Nineteen

Maxine

B Y THE TIME SHE finally got up the gumption to press the buzzer at the outer door to Nathan's swanky condo building, Maxine had talked herself out of several panic attacks. She hadn't been this nervous on her very *first* date. Hell, she hadn't even been this spun up on her wedding day.

Nathan's disembodied voice sounded through the speaker, "Come on up." The lock clicked, and she went inside.

As the elevator ascended, Maxine wiped her sweaty palms on the sides of her dress and willed herself to keep calm and stick with her plan. She had seduction in mind and had dressed accordingly. She was trimmed, plucked, waxed, pampered, perfumed, and ready. Screw dinner. She wanted Nathan naked and intended to have him that way.

When he opened his front door, the welcoming expression on his face disappeared as soon as he saw what she was wearing—a flame-red bodycon dress that left little to the imagination and her highest, sexiest stilettos.

Nathan's brow furrowed. "I thought I... I *did* tell you casual, right?"

"You did." Maxine felt a sliver of uncertainty and hesitated. Bewildered consternation wasn't what she was going for. She followed him inside, past a gorgeous living room to his spacious kitchen, where filled bowls and plates of every size and shape covered most of the surfaces. They ranged from tiny ramekins to oversize mixing bowls. In an instant, she understood that she'd played this all wrong. Tension settled in her stomach.

"I thought we'd make tapas." Still frowning, Nathan shifted his weight from one foot to the other. "It's something I've never made before. At first, I had the temptation to show off, but when is that ever a good idea? I figured learning together and good messy fun was better." He cast a glance around the room. "I only gathered the ingredients, no *mise en place*."

What the hell was *mise en place*? He was avoiding eye contact. Maxine wished the floor would open and swallow her up, but she pasted a bright smile on her face. "Sounds good. Let's get started. Where can I put my purse?"

Nathan hung it on a decorative hook by the front door, then produced a blue and white striped apron to protect her sequined cocktail dress. "What are you wearing?" he murmured, almost to himself as he tied the strings behind her.

"You don't like it?"

"I do, but... I don't want it to get ruined."

Even as foolish as she felt, Maxine could appreciate his thoughtfulness. All thoughts of seduction fled her mind, and self-consciousness took its place. "You won't judge my technique, will you?"

Nathan shook his head. "I never do that outside of work and only with someone I supervise. You're safe with me."

Maxine took in the variety of fresh foods while Nathan poured them both some sangria. "I've enjoyed tapas the few times I've had it."

"Good. Then let's get started."

Less than ten minutes in, they were absorbed in the recipes, and Maxine couldn't stop laughing. They swapped stories of various cooking triumphs and fiascos as they prepared gazpacho, gambas al ajillo, calamares fritos, empanadas, stuffed dates, mushroom croquettes, and more.

Maxine fanned herself as she took a sangria break while they waited for the stuffed mushrooms to finish. She'd ditched the high heels right away and tied her hair up out of the way with a scarf retrieved from her purse. "I once had a date where the guy said I was too good at everything. He found things I'd never done so he could teach me. It was awful."

Nathan stopped straining the beans that would go into the *espinacas con garbanzos* and cocked his head at her. "Why would he design an entire date around trying to humiliate you? That's asinine."

Maxine popped a marinated olive into her mouth as she pondered this. "I never thought of it that way. I thought he was just trying to impress me."

"Probably. But you shouldn't need to make someone feel like shit so you can show off."

The tapas were delicious and messy. The kitchen was a disaster by the time they finished their flan.

"Well, this is familiar," Nathan said, and Maxine chuckled.

Despite their best efforts, some of the tapas ended up on her dress. Nathan offered her one of his T-shirts. She removed the borrowed apron and faced away from him.

"You'll have to unzip me."

His breathing hitched as he pulled the tab down, revealing a lot of skin. She turned to face him and let the top of the dress slip down her arms to collect at her waist, revealing her sexiest bra. She almost laughed when his eyes bugged wide.

"Maxine—" His voice was raspy, close to a low growl.

There was fire in his eyes when their gazes collided. That was better. Maxine felt a quiver in her belly. Encouraged, she pushed the dress down over her hips. Before it could slither to the floor, his hand shot out to cover one of hers.

"Don't," he whispered.

Hurt and embarrassment were twin shocks to her system, like being doused in ice water. Maxine froze, then hurriedly straightened her dress, her cheeks burning. He'd been playful and flirtatious as they cooked, but... how had she gotten this so wrong? Tears were stinging the backs of her eyes. Oh, Lord, she was *not* going to cry over this. She refused. "I'll just go," she muttered. Why hadn't she scrapped this at the outset? She was reaching for the door when he took her by the elbows and drew her into him. "You don't have to say anything. It's okay. I'm just gonna—" *Slink away and die of humiliation.*

"Maxine." His voice was tender now, as was his touch when he cupped her chin to tilt her face up towards him. She couldn't meet his gaze. "I've jumped in too quickly in the past, and I don't want to do that here. Am I tempted? Good Lord, yes. You've been about two seconds away from being dragged off caveman-style since I opened the door."

Now Maxine looked up and saw the sincerity shining in his gaze. Some of her mortification faded. "So, the old it's not you, it's me?"

He smiled at her, and his smile was filled with warmth—affection, even. "It is completely me and not you."

Maxine suspected she could push the issue, but did she want Nathan to "give in", or did she want him to choose her? No one had ever been so conscientious about building something with her. The whole notion tugged at her heart.

Nathan Olivier might be more trouble than she thought.

Chapter Twenty

Nathan

ONE LOOK AT NATHAN and Tony Cuffee's eyebrows shot up almost to his hairline. Nathan had just arrived at the cemetery for their regular meetup. Tony declared, "Can't wait to hear this. Who is she?"

Nathan was tight-lipped and a little sullen as they trudged over the lush greens to Angel's grave. It was near sunset, her favorite time of day.

Together, Nathan and Tony cleared her headstone of the grass and other detritus that had accumulated since their last visit two months ago, then laid fresh flowers. Nathan had opted for a cheerful mix of multicolor gerbera daisies, while Tony went with her favorite sunflowers.

The jumble of emotions he always felt at the gravesite was... muted this time. Not quite as sharp. On their last visit, he had fought a blinding headache and a knot in his stomach.

Over a pepper pot dinner at one of their favorite restaurants, Nathan was pensive. He could feel Tony watching him and knew he'd keep after him until he spilled. So he did just that. Tony listened with rapt attention as Nathan told him about Maxine and the dates they'd had over the last several weeks.

Tony raised his coffee mug in salute. "She sounds great."

Picturing Maxine's wide smile, Nathan agreed. "She's fantastic."

"Then why are you moping?"

"I'm not moping." When Tony gave him the side-eye, Nathan huffed out a breath and shifted in his seat. "Okay, so I might be moping a little."

"You think Angel would have wanted you to blow off a chance at happiness? Like that's honoring her somehow? Or would she have read you the fucking riot act for moping in her name?"

The jab was so unexpected, so precise, it was like Tony stabbed him in the gut. Then twisted the knife. Nathan couldn't breathe for a moment. "That was low."

Tony was just getting started. "You think I can't tell you're hiding from commitment, son? You swung from one extreme to the other. I never pegged you for a coward."

"Don't," Nathan warned, shaking his head. "I'm already on edge."

"Then what's the problem? Is the sex bad or something?"

"We haven't had any. That's not the issue."

"Hold up." Tony sat his fork down on his plate. "You haven't slept with her? *You*?"

"No. She tried—" He broke off, unable to put into words what had happened the night they'd made tapas together. He'd scarcely touched her at all since, for fear of getting carried away. Jacking off every night wasn't providing nearly enough relief. "I almost gave myself a damn heart attack turning her down. I've got the blue balls to prove it."

Tony broke out into bawdy laughter, then held up a hand as he wheezed, his whole body shaking.

"Don't hurt anything laughing," Nathan snapped.

It took Tony several minutes to get himself under control. Before the chortles overtook him again, he asked, "What are you up to?"

Nathan said nothing.

Tony's gaze softened. "You think you don't deserve it?"

Nathan picked at the edge of his napkin and shifted in his chair. He *didn't* deserve it—several times over—and he was well aware of that fact.

"Now you listen here, Nathan." Tony's voice was low but sharp, commanding. All traces of conviviality were gone in a blink, and Nathan saw the ruthless prosecutor that defendants feared. "If you believe it should have been you instead of Angel—and I know damn well you do—then act like you got a second chance at life. Don't you dare disrespect her memory by sabotaging this."

With that, Tony sat back and regarded him with an introspective gaze, an eyebrow raised in challenge. *Your move, son,* his expression seemed to taunt.

Pieces clicked into place, and realization dawned. Nathan got to his feet in a hurry. "I gotta go." He pulled out his wallet, but Tony waved him off.

"Go handle your business. You get the next one and bring Maxine with you."

Chapter Twenty-One

Nathan

NATHAN DROVE STRAIGHT TO Maxine's house, and with blood rushing in his ears, he banged a fist on her door. He was poised to tell her everything when she answered, but then her eyes went wide and darted back inside. Her brow furrowed, and her lips pressed together in a grim line. "Nathan, this isn't a good time."

Nathan followed her gaze to spot the unmistakable profile of a guy with a bald head sitting in her living room. What he was going to say shriveled in his throat, and an almost violent urge ripped through him. He looked back at Maxine, who was chewing her lip and frowning. "I'd say I'm sorry I ruined your date, but I'd be lying my ass off."

"It's not a date."

"Funny, that sure looks like candlelight."

Maxine's face hardened. "Don't do the jealous bonehead bit. It's not attractive. I don't owe you an explanation. We're not even exclusive, remember?"

"Are you sleeping with him?" The question was out before he could consider the wisdom of asking it.

Maxine recoiled as if slapped, then jerked a thumb toward her driveway. "Get out. I don't have time to deal with possessive, irrational assholes."

Nathan grimaced and scratched the back of his neck. "Christ, I'm sorry. That was ignorant. I don't know what the hell I'm doing. I'm all twisted up here."

"And I'm not? You still don't get to act like a—"

"Possessive, irrational asshole. I know. I was way out of line with that. You're right, and I'm sorry."

She folded her arms. "If you recall, I threw myself at you a while ago. Don't worry, I got the message. I'm friend-zoned."

That brought him up short. "Is that what you think happened?"

"Isn't it?"

Crap. The jut of her chin told him the rest of the story. Nathan could have kicked himself. He just kept messing up with her.

"Ah, excuse me," a male voice said from behind Maxine. This time, when Nathan looked, belated recognition kicked in. It was her assistant, Dennis. The young man chewed his bottom lip, misery written on his face. "I'll just be going. Thanks for the advice, boss."

Nathan almost groaned. He was a dumbass of the highest order. He and Maxine watched Dennis get into his car and back out of her driveway.

When he turned back, Maxine's face had settled into a mask of fury. "This wasn't a date, was it?"

"No, it wasn't a date, you jerk!" She spat the words out at him and crossed her arms over her chest with a loud huff.

She was so damn pretty riled up, with her eyes snapping fire, but Nathan had damaged her trust in him. He was standing on a precipice. He palmed her face and brushed his lips against hers. After a brief hesitation, she responded, and Nathan could have jumped for joy.

Still cupping her face, Nathan forged ahead with determination. "When Angel died, I did every self-destructive thing I could think of. Rock climbing, bungee jumping, skydiving. Her widower came to see me and said I was being a jackass gambling with the gift I was given. When I saw him today, he reminded me of that and pointed out that I'd gone to the other extreme."

Her expression softened some. "What does that mean?"

"You are starting to matter to me, and I wasn't trying to mess that up. You're not friend-zoned. Not at all. I want to be exclusive with you." He stopped to take a breath and swallow hard. "I didn't want to just fall into bed with you by default. You have no goddamn idea how hard it was to resist when you tried to seduce me."

"Oh? Does this mean you're no longer resisting?"

He rested his forehead against hers and let out a shaky laugh. "No. Just say the word."

Instead of saying an actual word, Maxine stepped back to allow him inside. She closed the door behind him, then turned and led him down the hall. He followed, his heart thumping hard against his ribs. He felt like he was being lured into a den.

He hadn't been inside her bedroom before, but he didn't spare more than a minimal glance around. Only to the massive four-poster bed, then back at the gorgeous creature before him. He waved a hand at her. "All of it—*off*." His voice was gruff as he toed off his shoes and kicked them aside.

"You're issuing orders again," she teased, but she grasped the hem of her dress as she said it. She hauled the whole thing up and over her head and let it drop, revealing an almost see-through teal bra and panty set.

Jesus, the *curves*. Nathan yanked his T-shirt off and tossed it aside. Maxine unhooked her bra but cupped her breasts to keep it from falling away. The teal color was striking against her dark skin. He liked the way her admiring gaze skimmed over his bare upper body. Nathan might not be in the same peak physical condition as his Elite Guard days, but he'd kept in pretty good shape. "You going to do as I say?"

Her half-smile was full of impishness. "I might." She let go of the bra, and with a little shimmy, it slid down her arms and fluttered to the floor. "You wanted to kiss and suck these, right?"

Nathan forgot how to breathe for a moment. *Dear Lord.* This woman was going to bring him to his knees. Her pouty nipples were like two black cherries, erect and begging for his attention. Instead of removing her panties the way he expected, she slipped her fingers down into the front of them and stroked herself. *Aw, hell.*

The last fine thread of Nathan's restraint was already threatening to snap. Watching Maxine get herself off would be too damned much for any mortal. Mischief was gleaming in her eyes, as was a teensy bit of challenge. Maxine turned her back to him to ease her mesh panties down, one tortuous millimeter at a time. It riveted Nathan. She bent at the waist, and he almost growled when he got his first glimpse of her pretty, perfect pussy. She stepped out of the panties and dropped them aside as she turned to face him again.

Nathan almost lost control right then. She was luscious. So goddamn perfect, standing there before him, confident and proud. Nathan wanted to devour her.

"On the bed." His voice was hoarse even to his own ears. His cock was hard enough to bust steel. Maxine took her time arranging herself, lying back on the pillows with her thighs spread just enough to flash him another peek at her lovely pussy.

He crawled up over her body, nestling between her legs. It was a delicious tease feeling the heat of her core, right where he most wanted to be. Nathan palmed one of her breasts and leaned in to brush his lips against her taut nipple. She drew in a sharp breath, then uttered a breathy cry of protest when he stopped just short of pulling it into his mouth. She arched her back, willing him to do it. Oh, she was going to be so much fun to tease.

Nathan ground against her and fought the urge to hurry so he could slake his thirst for her. He had business to take care of here first. He had pleasure to give and the landscape of her body to study. "I'll need you to trust me."

"We wouldn't be in my bed if I didn't trust you."

The simple words were a balm to his soul. Hovering above her, he felt a ripple of exhilaration as she skated her fingertips up his sides. She took two fistfuls of his locs and pulled his mouth down to hers. Her impatience was like a drug in his system, fogging his mind.

At last, she was his to touch, taste, and sample. When she'd had her delectable ass in the air a minute ago, it was all he could do to not drop to his knees and worship at her altar. *Next time.*

Nathan nuzzled the crook of her neck and nipped her earlobe. "God, woman, the things I want to do to you."

He relished her shiver. Nathan got to work on his single objective of driving her wild. There was no rush, and he had nothing but patience to earn the coveted reward of her release. He focused on exploring every curve and plane of her magnificent body. So much tantalizing softness and fragrant skin to discover, to investigate. Nathan did his best to catalog every detail—every telltale sound, each movement, where she was ticklish, and what made her sigh or catch her lip between her teeth.

Her uninhibited responses were the biggest turn-on. Everything about her revved Nathan up. Maxine watched him as he kissed, nibbled, and prepared. The naked desire glimmering in her eyes almost undid him. Such desire for him, for *this.*

Nathan came close to losing it again when he found her trimmed curls wet. He let out an appreciative groan as he stroked his fingertips through the evidence of her excitement. His first taste of her sweetness almost finished him. He sensed the tension gathering within her and went after it, following her cues. She trembled and came apart after a long climb, and he nearly let loose a whoop of triumph.

Chapter Twenty-Two

Maxine

HE JUST KEPT SURPRISING her. Teasing him was fun, feeling his delicious gaze on her, heavy with want. Those lips on her throat were enough to send heat zinging through her. She thought she'd lose her mind when he kissed and sucked each nipple in turn. He wasn't gentle; he was demanding and bossy, but oh, so very attentive.

His long, broad fingers manipulated her flesh, eliciting laughter when he discovered ticklish spots she didn't even know she had. His mouth was addictive. When he whispered to her that she was beautiful, Maxine had never felt more so than she did then. Her fingers itched to touch him, but she faltered when she tried, for it was impossible to concentrate on trying to touch him. Her brain and body couldn't split her attention that way at all.

Nathan lifted his head from the glorious things he was doing between her legs, and his eyes were blazing. "Put your hands on the headboard and keep them there."

So he wanted complete dominion over her. It was so hot, so unexpected, Maxine wasn't sure what to feel beyond a titillated excitement shooting through her. Between the order itself and the strident tone of voice, everything in her responded. She raised her hands above her head to grip the slats. She'd never felt so exposed and would have thought she'd dislike it. But he looked over the length of her like she was a feast, and he was starving.

He made a careful study of her body, as though he had all the time in the world just to make her weak and delirious with pleasure. The unhurried exploration was thorough and wreaked absolute havoc on her senses. His teasing was skillful. He kept making incremental adjustments based on her reactions until she was ready to weep in exquisite anticipation.

He uncovered her secrets; some she didn't even know she was keeping.

Nathan nibbled and stroked his way down her body to push her legs open wider to accommodate his broad shoulders. His eyes were dark and serious as he caressed the outside of her thigh and left a hot, lingering kiss on the sensitive skin of her knee. Maxine let her breath out in a hiss when he, at last, gave her a long, slow lick up her seam and her clit a gentle suck. He lashed it with his tongue at a languid pace, emitting a low sound in the back of his throat. His licking, sucking, and nibbling drove her wild. She couldn't remain still beneath the onslaught. He stayed slow, building her pleasure with painstaking attention.

His name was an incantation as her first orgasm slammed into her like a freight train. Maxine moaned, every nerve ending on fire as she twisted and undulated under him. She kept a tight grip on the headboard, though it may have been the hardest thing she'd ever done. But the restriction sharpened the pleasure in a way she didn't expect.

He rode the crest of bliss with her until she stopped shuddering, then did it again. He sank a finger inside her to stroke there while he used his thumb, then his tongue, to circle her clit. Maxine cried out, her hips bucking up against him. Oh, Lord, she was going to come again, this time right into his mouth. He grabbed her hips, and she lost herself in the determination in his eyes. When she flew over the edge this time, they maintained eye contact, and it was the hottest thing Maxine had ever done.

Nathan flowed to his feet next to the bed, and his expression was fierce. Maxine released the headboard's slats and rose to her elbows to get a better view of him.

"Trust me," he whispered, reaching for the button of his jeans. Maxine nodded and fell back into the pillows.

She wanted to lick the trail of fine hair at his lower abdomen, where it disappeared into his remaining clothing. He shoved his pants and boxer briefs down and off, giving her the full monty. Maxine tilted her head as she took him in, admiring his beauty. Her ardent gaze slid from his face, over his chest and torso down to his erect cock. And there her wandering gaze stalled, and she let out an involuntary gasp.

No wonder he was telling her to trust him. His cock was *huge*—both long and thick, jutting away from his body. And with a pearl of pre-come glistening at the tip. Renewed heat pooled in Maxine's belly.

He saw her staring. "Don't worry about this."

How could she not be a little intimidated? She'd never been with someone so well-endowed. Maxine didn't know if she wanted to drool or run, but the aching emptiness within her was growing. "Uh—"

Nathan stroked himself, and the motion of those long, elegant fingers gliding up and down his shaft mesmerized her. "Trust me, Maxine. You'll be ready for me."

He retrieved his wallet from his discarded pants and pulled out a slim container that, at first glance, seemed to be a credit card. But it opened, and Nathan pulled out a condom packet.

Clever. Maxine always hated reading in romance novels about men whipping condoms out of their wallets—one of the least safe places to store them. Of course, she had some in her goodie drawer, but she wasn't confident they would fit him. Nathan kept his eyes on hers as he rolled the condom on. Then he was back on the bed and using his tongue on her—slowly—just the way she liked, making her even more greedy for him. He didn't instruct her to put her hands on the headboard again. All thoughts of uncertainty fled with the dizzying circles he was making around her clit. Then she was coming again.

By the time he used the head of his cock to nudge her slickened opening, Maxine was so damn ready for him she nearly cried. At the same time, she wanted to retreat, but he held her in place and cupped her chin while he gazed deep into her eyes as he fed her his cock. An apprehensive whimper escaped, even as she stretched and yielded to accept him. Nathan was all comfort and persistence, though. He pulled away some and gave her more of him with a steady advance, covering her body with his. When she squirmed and tensed, he lifted her hips, used his muscular thighs to spread hers a little farther apart, and filled her again. Maxine closed her eyes against the overwhelming sensations, but the rumble of his sonorous voice chased her.

"Eyes on me, sweetheart."

Her eyes flew open to lock on his. That golden-brown gaze was so intense, so full of heat. Could she do this? "Nathan, I—"

"You can take it. Stay with me."

"You're going to break me," she hissed through clenched teeth.

"Never, love. Trust me. We're almost there." He sucked one of her nipples hard, bringing her back arching off the bed. He advanced a little farther as he kissed and soothed the stiffened point. And so it went, him distracting her with his touch.

Finally, they were flush. Maxine had never felt so full. He held them there for a long, blissful moment and brushed his lips against the sensitive spot below her earlobe. Tension coiled, and heat built at her core again.

"Look at how well you take me. Ah, Maxine, you're perfect."

His words stirred something primal buried within her, and Maxine needed more. He was holding back, but she was ready for him to *move*. She tightened her channel and curled her limbs around him to draw him closer. She sighed his name into the juncture of his neck and shoulder.

It was like a dam breaking. The careful control he'd been exerting fell away. Finesse flew out the window, leaving them grasping and clutching at each other. Their need and raw hunger were colliding, their bodies slipping and sliding together.

He angled into her to ride over the precious spot he'd found earlier with his fingers. The weight of him pressed his pelvis onto her clit with each thrust. He stayed attuned to her slightest reaction and must have seen it, for he stopped to grind onto her. It made her almost lose her mind. Maxine clamped her knees around his hips and arched, losing control. He murmured encouragement as she burst around him. His eyes on hers were full of fire. He gave her no reprieve, drove into her hard and deep again and again as she mewled and thrashed.

His voice was there with her, almost a physical entity, though she was beyond comprehending the words. Maxine clung to his hard body as his thrusts sped, somehow both easing and stoking that visceral ache only he could fulfill. Her breathing hitched as her body strained. It was too much. She was too sensitive. She needed—there was no way she could—

"Do it." He growled the command, and her body responded.

The world broke apart as she peaked once more. Maxine lapsed into inarticulate moans and cries, barely able to hang onto him. Nathan's hold on her tightened. He speared all the way home and went rigid, releasing a heavy groan as he, too, came.

Breathing hard and spent, they lay entangled.

Nathan pushed up on his elbows and kissed her. Maxine gave a long, satisfied sigh as he withdrew from her. She didn't remember dozing off, but Nathan had to shake her awake by the shoulder.

"Come. I drew you a bath."

Maxine sat up and swung her legs over the edge of the bed. "You did?" She took the hand he held out and stood. She flinched, feeling their tight fit between her legs.

Nathan took her face in his hand and kissed her lips lightly. "I'm sorry. The bath will help."

They soaked together in her enormous jacuzzi tub, Maxine sitting between his legs, leaning back against his chest. Something deep within seemed to melt when he pressed a lingering kiss to her temple. She'd been prepared for a raunchy, expletive-laden romp, not this care, this incredible tenderness. Although she should have known Nathan would never go for the obvious. She'd likely be sore tomorrow, but it would be worth it.

Chapter Twenty-Three

Nathan

T HE UNIVERSITY FRESHMAN SHOWCASE kept Nathan busy for the next few weeks. In between teaching master classes, the one-on-one coaching, judging challenges, and publicity, he didn't have nearly enough time to spend lingering with Maxine—in bed or out. They maximized any time they had.

While he wouldn't have ever described himself as sappy, Nathan was happier than he could ever remember being. He surprised Maxine with a quick off-island hop to a bed and breakfast, where they did nothing but relax and soak each other up for a weekend.

A text from Ericka came in while they were away, and Nathan teared up over the ultrasound image. Maxine knelt behind where he was sitting and slid her arms around him in an affectionate squeeze. They were both still naked, basking in each other and the afternoon warmth.

"Are they going to find out the baby's sex?"

Nathan shook his head. "They want to be surprised."

"I've been working on some fun ideas for her layette. This is going to be one stylish baby."

Nathan marveled at her. "Previous partners seemed to think they were in competition with Ericka."

Maxine gave a snort of derision. "That's absurd. She's your daughter. There's never going to be any competition there."

Her no-nonsense assessment was so matter-of-fact, a flare of heat and emotion sizzled through his synapses. Maxine was always going to have his back.

He loved her.

The knowledge slammed into Nathan, and he'd never felt anything so profound.

Sudden, voracious desire raced through him. Nathan flipped his woman onto her back and got his mouth busy between her thighs. When she was out of her mind with ecstasy, he rolled on a condom and sank inside her as deep as her luscious body would allow, all in a single thrust. Maxine welcomed him inside her slick perfection with a sigh of his name. They'd made love enough that she'd gotten accustomed to taking him inside her heat more easily. This time, he didn't give her a chance to catch her breath.

Maxine was wild beneath him, all softness and liquid warmth. She tightened her legs around his thighs and leveraged herself upward to meet him at the top of each stroke. She was gorgeous, the most beautiful thing he'd ever seen.

He loved her.

Nathan thrust hard with the sudden clarity, pulling a euphoric cry from her. "Tell me you're mine, Maxine."

She reached for him. He took her hand and kissed her palm. The intimacy of it made his chest hurt.

"You would claim me?"

"Every single day, if you'll let me."

Tears filled her eyes, and her voice was thick with emotion. "I am yours, Nathan. All yours."

The weight and enormity of it all were almost more than Nathan could bear. He closed his eyes to let the tide of all he was feeling wash over him. Then he pushed them hard to a shattering climax.

Later, once they'd come down from the high, Maxine snuggled in close to his side and he wrapped an arm around her.

"Well, that was intense." She was stroking her fingers over his stomach. "Where did that come from? Are you alright?"

He kissed her forehead, just the barest brush of his lips against her skin. "Never better, lovely."

An idea was already forming.

Once they'd dressed for dinner, Nathan told Maxine to go ahead downstairs to order their drinks. "I'll be right there. Gotta do one quick thing." He was already dialing his cell phone by the time the door closed behind her.

"Chef Nathan." The voice on the other end was cheerful as always. "To what do I owe the pleasure?"

"I only have a minute, but I need you to listen to me very carefully."

Chapter Twenty-Four

Maxine

"**S**OMETHING ON YOUR MIND?" Dennis asked.

"No. What makes you ask?" A week had passed since the glorious weekend away with Nathan. Maxine was still walking on air.

Dennis pointed at her lap. "That doesn't look like a gown."

"What?" Maxine looked down. Indeed, her sketchpad was full of random shapes and swirls and *hearts*, for heaven's sake. "Oh, no. I'm sorry. I don't know where my mind is."

Okay, that was a flat-out lie. Maxine knew precisely where her mind was. It was on remembering how Nathan had bent her over the bathroom counter and made love to her with slow, deliberate strokes—driving her to a climax so powerful and all-consuming she'd nearly passed out.

"Is everything okay, boss? You've been sort of out of it lately."

And then him handing her a mug of her favorite tea and a plate of freshly baked scones and winking at her? His knowing gaze raking her body was more intimate than a caress. Pure heaven.

No wonder she loved him.

Maxine struggled to take a breath. With blood rushing in her ears, she clutched a hand to her chest. Dimly, she heard Dennis' panicked voice asking if she was okay, but she was up and pacing. The notebook tumbled to the floor.

Now wait a minute. In *love*? Was she?

Her feelings had been building for a while. Even now, as she thought of him, everything within her softened.

Maxine turned that over in her mind, the fluttery feeling back in her stomach. That same fluttery feeling she always seemed to have when she thought of Nathan. In the months they'd been dating, that zip of excitement, like being at the crest of a roller coaster, was still there.

It wasn't just the sex, although making love with Nathan was enough to change anyone's worldview. She slept better when she was in his arms. Hell, *everything* was better with Nathan in her life. But... *love*?

Oh, sweet Caroline, she *was* in love. Maxine gasped.

As if reading her thoughts, Dennis said, "If he's in your heart, then he's in your heart. Don't let your head get in the way. That's the advice you gave me."

It was what she'd advised Dennis just before Nathan had shown up that night they'd made love for the first time. Maxine stopped her pacing and faced the notion head-on this time.

She was in love with Nathan. This time, joy blossomed in her chest with the thought. Maxine pictured the warmth in Nathan's eyes and smile from that morning and gave a giddy laugh. The hot chef had made her fall in love with him. How about that?

"When you picture yourself ten years from now, do you see him there with you?"

"Absolutely." Maxine couldn't imagine a day without Nathan.

"Tell him how you feel. Then figure it out together."

Maxine looked at her protégé, her heart swelling with pride at how much he'd matured in their time together. "When did you get so wise?"

Dennis grinned at her. "I had an excellent mentor."

"You're a gem, Dennis. I'll tell him when I see him tonight."

The day took a turn when Dennis received a phone call that rattled him. He grew antsy and kept checking his watch so often that Maxine finally asked him what was up. His unconvincing *nothing* just had her tapping her foot and giving him a skeptical look.

"Don't look at me like that," he pleaded. "I have one job to do, and it's almost time."

"What the heck?"

"Please don't ask me any questions. You know I'm a terrible liar, and this is super important."

He looked so stressed out that Maxine took pity on him. "Okay, without telling me anything about it, what do you need me to do?"

He didn't need her to do much, just work on something she could put aside in about an hour. She was to stay off her phone and computer. No text, no emails, no Internet. The poor kid was sweating bullets, so Maxine agreed without argument, even though she was itching to ask an avalanche of questions.

At the top of the hour, a relieved-looking Dennis clicked on the television and flopped down into a chair. Maxine didn't ask questions, just nudged her notebook aside and waited. *Good Afternoon Lytua* was entering its second half, and just before a commercial break, one of the hosts teased an upcoming segment with special guest Chef Nathan Olivier.

Maxine laughed at the cloak-and-dagger drama, leaning back in her desk chair. "Is that all? He does this kind of thing all the—" She broke off at Dennis' beseeching look. Nathan hadn't even told her he was going to be guest-starring. If he had, she would have made it a point to watch. Dennis looked as though he was going to be ill any second. Why would Nathan insist her assistant get her to watch?

A different host gave the lead-in after the break, announcing that he'd had a chance to catch up with the all-star chef a few days ago. It was a meaty profile about his work—nothing unusual, just great publicity. Maxine couldn't help but smile when Nathan walked through how to make her favorite conch fritters.

In the voiceover, the host said, "And then there was this bombshell."

On-screen, the host was still following Nathan around the Queen's kitchen. "So, did I hear this correctly? You might be off the market?"

Maxine's breath caught. Nathan grinned, a full-on megawatt smile that made her belly quiver.

"Yes, that's correct. If she'll have me. I fell in love with an extraordinary woman. I wasn't looking for it, but Maxine is all I ever wanted in a woman."

He was still talking, but Maxine was bawling all of a sudden and hardly heard a word of it. Nathan had just told the entire world he was in love with her. He loved her! Maxine was swamped with emotion, and a happy lightness filled her soul.

Throughout Nathan talking about falling in love, compromising, and making things work, Maxine listened with tears in her eyes.

Dennis was grinning from ear to ear. She gave him a bone-crushing hug and thanked him. No way was she waiting until tonight to confess her feelings.

Halfway to the Hub, Maxine remembered Nathan was teaching an intensive today at the community center. She plugged the address into the GPS and changed course.

It was easy enough to find the classroom, although Maxine didn't see Nathan anywhere when she walked in. She cleared her throat to raise her voice above the din. "Excuse me, I'm looking for Chef Nathan Olivier."

A young man cupped his hands and yelled out, "Yo, Chef, there's a babe here to see you!"

Nathan popped up from where he'd been squatting next to the demo range at the front of the classroom, a red whisk in his hand. His face split into a wide smile for her. "Oh, hello. Class, this is—"

"So, you love me?" Maxine interrupted, the question sounding more like a challenge.

Nathan sat the utensil down on the counter, put his hands on his hips, and met her with a level gaze. "I do. Is that going to be a problem?"

Maxine strode over to Nathan, threw her arms around his neck, and kissed him with all the affection and adoration that had welled up in her. The students whistled and cheered around them.

"Yes, I most certainly will have you. I love you, too."

He wrapped her up and pulled her close. "I'm talking about getting married, you know. Just so we're clear. Buying a house, maybe getting a dog or two."

"Yes. Yes, to everything. I want a cat, too."

"Whatever you want."

They pulled apart after another kiss, laughing at the furor it caused among the students.

"All right, all right, everyone, simmer down." Nathan leaned in to whisper in her ear. "I'll see you later at my house."

Maxine couldn't contain her smirk. "I'll bring champagne."

The End

Need more Maxine and Nathan?
Get an **exclusive bonus epilogue to *A Matter of Taste*** when you join my reader list!
Sign up here!

A Matter of Taste Bonus Epilogue

If the sparks, banter, or kitchen heat made you smile, swoon, or crave more, I'd be so grateful if you shared your thoughts in a review.

Reviews help more than you know and only take a minute.

Leave a review here.

A Matter of Taste Reviews

Start with *International Incident*
Crown & Heart, Book 1

The queen swore her heart to duty alone.

Can he be the exception to her rule?

Begin the story that started it all—

royal intrigue, slow-burn heat,

and a love that could change the fate of a nation.

Available now.

International Incident

Before *International Incident* and *Queen of His Heart*,
Sparks flew with Jaden and Aimee....

In the Queen's Service (Crown & Heart Book 3) transports readers to the turbulent early days of Khara Therin's reign. Before Jaden Everly was the devoted husband and father we know and love, he was a grumpy, inflexible know-it-all too used to being in charge.

He's juggling national security and a royal transition, with zero time —or interest—for romance.

Until Dr. Aimee Sebastien dances into his life at his brother's wedding and makes it very clear she isn't here to be impressed.

Challenge accepted.

Coming soon—join my newsletter so you don't miss the release.

In the Queen's Service

NIKKI DAVENPORT IS A contemporary romance and romantic suspense author and the creator of the Crown & Heart/Destination: Lytua series—where Wakanda meets *Bridgerton* in a lush, all-Black world of royal romance and unapologetic joy. Her stories reimagine royalty through high-stakes emotion, deep friendships, and characters who fight for love and legacy.

Her debut novel, *International Incident*, became an Amazon bestseller, ranking in the Top 15 of Romantic Suspense and Top 55 of Contemporary Romance, and was selected as a 2023 finalist for the Audio in Color Award. Book two in the series went on to hit #1 in Black & African American Women's Fiction, launching a royal universe readers can't wait to return to.

A lifelong lover of love stories, Nikki holds a BA in History and a Master's in Social Work. She is also the founder of Granite Clover Publishing, LLC, and Granite Clover Author Services, a boutique author-services company offering culturally responsive manuscript support for fiction and nonfiction writers. She works in education by day, paddles with a dragon boat team of fellow breast cancer survivors in her off time, and belongs to a fabulous book club. She lives in Northern Virginia with her husband, a snarky teen, and two spoiled feline overlords—and is rarely without an audiobook or podcast.

Nikki is passionately committed to centering Black love on the page—and isn't stopping anytime soon.

Follow her on Goodreads (37165373.Nikki_Davenport), Book Bub (@nikkidavenportauthor), and Facebook (AuthorNikkiDavenport)!

Also by Nikki Davenport

The Crown & Heart Series

International Incident — Crown & Heart Book 1

A Matter of Taste — A Crown & Heart Novella (Book 1.5)

Queen of His Heart — Crown & Heart Book 2

Season of the Heart — A Crown & Heart Prequel (Book 3)

In the Queen's Service — Crown & Heart Book 3

Worth the Risk — A Crown & Heart Prequel (Book 4)

Healing Reign — Crown & Heart Book 4

Fool Me Once — A Crown & Heart Novella

Also Appearing in Anthologies

Courage: An Anthology to Kick Cancer's Ass — "A Matter of Taste"

Holly & Heartstrings Holiday Anthology — "Season of the Heart"

Crown & Heart Series Guide